Dear Romance Reader,

Welcome to a world of breathtaking passion and never-ending romance.
Welcome to *Precious Gem Romances.*

It is our pleasure to present *Precious Gem Romances,* a wonderful new line of romance books by some of America's best-loved authors. Let these thrilling historical and contemporary romances sweep you away to far-off times and places in stories that will dazzle your senses and melt your heart.

Sparkling with joy, laughter, and love, each *Precious Gem Romance* glows with all the passion and excitement you expect from the very best in romance. Offered at a great affordable price, these books are an irresistible value—and an essential addition to your romance collection. Tender love stories you will want to read again and again, *Precious Gem Romances* are books you will treasure forever.

Look for eight fabulous new *Precious Gem Romances* each month—available only at Wal★Mart.

Lynn Brown, Publisher

COURTING TROUBLE

Nancy Fraser

Zebra Books
Kensington Publishing Corp.

http://www.zebrabooks.com

For Robb and Kevin, my heart and my soul;

For the Critiquettes, Lisa Drummond, Marianne Evans and Debbie Lampi, who make writing (and rewriting!) a pleasure and friendship an art;

And for Alexander who, by setting me free, gave me wings and taught me to fly!

ZEBRA BOOKS are published by

Kensington Publishing Corp.
850 Third Avenue
New York, NY 10022

First Printing: November, 1996
10 9 8 7 6 5 4 3 2 1

Printed in the United States of America

One

This, Jessi decided, *is the most humiliating experience I've ever had to endure in all my twenty-four years.*

Hadn't she come to the sheriff's office willingly?

She hadn't been arrested; she hadn't been forced to ride in the back of their brown and white patrol car. Yet, despite her willingness to help, she was being treated like a child. And, to top it all off, they didn't believe her.

The cigar-chomping, know-it-all deputy had openly implied that she'd fabricated the entire story. If only Mrs. Chalmers hadn't lost her glasses. If only . . .

"Excuse me, Miss, I'm Sheriff Logan. Dane Logan."

Jessi looked up, her gaze clashing with the bluest eyes she'd ever seen. The face they graced wasn't bad either—if you like the handsome type. The tall, Nordic blond, handsome type. Jessi could feel her temperature rising. Encouraged by Sheriff Logan's slow smile, her pulse raced.

"I'm Jessi Trainor. I've come to file a report on an incident that happened earlier today."

Dane lifted the deputy's hastily scribbled report from the desk, his gaze scanning the page while his thoughts were on the girl in the chair. She was different. Cute. Young. Too young.

Automatically, he moved on to the section devoted to information on the complainant. Twenty-four. No way. She didn't look a day over eighteen.

"Miss Trainor, I'd like for you to repeat your story one more time."

"Is that necessary, Sheriff? I've been over my statement at least six times. Your deputies seem to be highly amused by it."

Dane rubbed the bridge of his nose. Sighing, he settled into the chair behind his desk. What had happened to his day off? It had ended the minute he'd received Pike's call. His peace of mind had evaporated shortly thereafter—with his first look at Jessi Trainor.

"I'm sorry, Miss Trainor, but it's necessary. I'll do my best to be as expeditious as possible."

She nodded, her smile no more than a fleeting quirk of her full, pink-tinged lips.

"Could you start at the beginning, please?"

Rather loudly, she cleared her throat. Dane suspected she was embarrassed. Yet, without hearing it in her own words, he couldn't determine the validity of her complaint. Besides, he noted rather unwillingly, he liked listening to her talk. Her husky voice was at odds with her fragile frame. Her voice belonged to a tall, busty blonde, not a diminutive redhead.

"I left my apartment about noon," she began. "I live at the Patterson's on Elmwood. In the apartment upstairs."

He nodded.

"Mrs. Chalmers asked me to call for her on my way into town. She has trouble seeing, even with her glasses, and wanted me to walk with her. We'd reached the corner of Maple and Fourth when this man stepped out from beside Breezer's Bar and Grill.

"Did he say anything?"

"No. He had this ridiculous grin on his face—but evil, like the Joker in *Batman*. I thought maybe he was going to mug us."

The thought of someone so small fending off a mugger

sent both his protective instincts and his urge to lecture into overdrive.

"What happened next?" he asked.

"He stopped right in front of us. I thought, at first, Miss Chalmers knew him by the way she smiled. But then I realized, she smiles at everyone. That was when he did it."

"Did it?"

"Yeah, he opened his coat and flashed us."

Dane quickly stifled the urge to laugh. "Go on," he prompted.

"I screamed . . . I think. Then I threw my hands up and covered Miss Chalmers's eyes. A sight like that could give an old lady the vapors. I'm afraid I knocked her glasses off and broke them. I'm really sorry about that."

"Did Miss Chalmers see the man before you broke her glasses?"

"I don't think so. She says she didn't see anybody." Biting nervously on her thumbnail, Jessi asked, "Did I say I was sorry about breaking her glasses?"

"Yes," he assured her, "you did."

"Oh. Good."

"Can you describe the man?" Dane asked.

"Yes. He was Caucasian, about five-foot-nine or ten. Brown hair, brown eyes. Approximately thirty-years-old. He had a scar on his right cheek."

Dane's previous urge to laugh was quickly replaced by anger toward the man who had upset and embarrassed Jessi Trainor. Unlike his deputies, he believed her story. "Anything else?" he asked.

"No, nothing else."

"Was he naked from the waist down?"

"Yes."

"Were there any identifying marks on his legs or on his—"

"I don't know," she said quickly, nervously. "I didn't look close enough . . . I mean . . . I . . . averted my eyes. I concentrated on his face and coat."

The blush that crept into Jessi Trainor's cheeks was beguiling. His gaze lingering on her rose-shaded skin, Dane asked, "His coat?"

"Yes. He was wearing a four-hundred-dollar Simons and Rail raincoat. His shoes were expensive, as well. Bassliner wingtips."

"You seem to know a lot about clothes. How come?"

"I worked my way through college as a men's clothing buyer for a large department store chain."

"What did you study in college?" The question was unimportant to his investigation, but relevant to his personal need for information about Jessi Trainor.

"I majored in Home Economics and minored in English Lit. I'd planned on opening my own catering business someday."

"And did you?"

She shook her head.

"Why not?"

"I got sidetracked."

When she didn't offer anything further, he asked, "Sidetracked by what?"

"Another career. I write cookbooks. I'm working on my third one now. That's why I'm here in Brant County."

"Brant County in a cookbook?"

"Yes. I'm using Michigan's abundant varieties of cherries and other fruits as a basis for an entire section on no-fat desserts, muffins, and breads."

"And you're doing this in the apartment above Abel Patterson's house?"

"Yes," she said enthusiastically. As quickly as it had come, her smile faded, and she asked, "Is that okay? It's not against some ordinance, is it?"

Dane noted a thread of anxiousness and genuine uncertainty in her question. He shook his head. "No, Miss Trainor, you're not upsetting anything."

Except my equilibrium.

"Is there anything else, Sheriff? I've got an appointment with Clara Severs at three. She's going to give me her recipe for Cherry Surprise."

Dane spared a moment's thought for Clara's Cherry Surprise.

He licked his lips, and immediately felt the warmth of Jessi Trainor's gaze on his mouth. "That's a great recipe," he told her. "I've enjoyed a dish or two myself over the years."

"Have you lived around here long?" she asked.

"Most my life. I grew up giving old Sheriff Keates fits. I never thought for one minute during all those years, I'd one day have his job, and that I'd be looking after old friends, while making new ones."

Unexplainably, the air around them seem to thicken, their gazes met and melded comfortably. Dane sensed something special in Jessi Trainor—something not easily ignored. When she smiled, he returned the meek gesture with a broad one of his own.

"Anything else?" she asked a second time.

"Just one more question."

She nodded, the subtle movement of her head causing her bright red hair to shine with golden highlights.

"Are you really twenty-four?"

Her sigh was audible, the resignation in the throaty sound telling him without words that she'd been doubted many times before. "Twenty-four years, four months, and six days to be exact."

Bracing his hands flat on the desk, Dane stood and stared down at her. "No more questions, Miss Trainor. You're free to go."

She stood as well, the top of her head barely reaching his breastbone. Measured against his own six-foot-two, he guessed her to be five-foot-one at the most. And ninety-five pounds soaking wet—if she was lucky. Still, despite her diminutive size, she exuded a quiet inner strength and determination. And, he noted somewhat reluctantly, a hyperactive innocence he found most attractive.

As she gathered her things, she asked, "What will be done about my report?"

"We'll keep an eye out for the man. Although, he sounds like he might be a stranger just passing through. He's probably a hundred miles away, or more, by now."

"What should I do if I see him again?"

"Call me. I'll be handling your complaint myself."

Jessi shifted her weight from one foot to the other, realigning the heavy grocery bag in her arms. As she fumbled with the lock, the key fell out of her hand and through the crack in the porch, landing on the ground one flight below.

"Oh . . . darn." Setting the grocery bag down on the small landing, she trudged down the stairs to retrieve the key. "Silly twit," she admonished herself. "If you'd had your mind on business you'd have set the bag down first. But no, not you. You couldn't think that straight. Could you?" Shaking her head, she continued, "No, you gotta be thinking about Sheriff Logan."

Just the mention of his name—even from her own lips— caused her steps to falter. She'd thought of nothing else since earlier that day. Clara Severs, she was sure, had given up on any hope of intelligent conversation half way through their interview. No matter how hard she'd tried, Jessi hadn't been able to marshall her thoughts into line. No matter how much Clara had talked about picking cherries and preparing good food, Jessi had thought of only the blonde-haired, blue-eyed, sheriff.

Picking the keys up off the ground, she grasped the railing and started to climb. What the heck was wrong with her anyway? He was just a man, after all. She'd dated men before. Well . . . boys really. When compared to Dane Logan, every man she'd ever known was nothing more than a boy.

Checking the directions one last time, Jessi slid the cookie sheet into the middle of the oven, then sat down on a nearby chair and buried her face in her hands. "Well, so much for cooking therapy. That didn't help a bit." Glancing down at her bare feet and silky pajamas, she shook her head. "Even cooking can't take your mind off Sheriff Logan. Face it, Jessi, you're a lost cause. A goner."

One hour and four dozen cookies later, Jessi cleaned up her bowls and spoons and washed down the small stove. It was barely nine-thirty. She couldn't face the thought of going to bed so early. She was lonely, and she missed her evening gab sessions with Abel and Erline Patterson. Although she'd been in Brant Mills less than two months, she'd become quite fond of her landlord and his wife. She'd come to count on their company during the long summer evenings. She'd come to expect them to entertain her.

Wrong.

Addressing her reflection in the window pane, she asked, "Jessi, when are you going to grow up? You're a big girl now. There are no coaches, no trainers, no over-protective parents, no one waiting on you hand and foot." Brushing back her unruly red curls, she sighed. "No one to give a darn whether you ever do anything of value again."

She moved restlessly around the kitchen, driven by pent-up energy, and a frustration she didn't understand. Crossing the room, she opened the window overlooking the roof above the Patterson's sun porch. To the left of the roof was a young oak tree. The tree housed two families of birds whose cheerful morning songs had quickly become her alarm clock.

Leaning out the window, she surveyed the yard. Twilight had settled in, throwing a hazy moonlit glow over everything. From time to time, the clouds shifted, their fuzzy thickness blanketing the moon and casting eerie shadows into the yard. The calm day had turned into a breezy evening, the lightweight wind buffeting the tree's branches.

Drawing a deep draft of air, Jessi surveyed the yard one last time. That was when she saw it. The baby bird. He'd fallen from his nest and landed on the roof. "Oh, you poor baby," she crooned. "I'll save you. Hang on a minute."

Jessi slipped on her canvas running shoes and climbed through the window. Inching her way closer and closer to the tiny, featherless bird, she mumbled phrases of encouragement, more for herself than the chick. She slipped twice, managing at the last minute to secure her footing and avoid a fall. Her concentration solely on the bird, she lifted him from the roof and returned him to his nest. "There you go, little chirper. Safe and sound."

On her hands and knees, she negotiated the shingled roof. Just short of the window, she stood. The wind gusted suddenly, knocking her off balance. With a grace earned from years of Olympic-level gymnastics training, and without conscious thought, she compensated for the breeze, regaining her balance and returning to an upright stance. Unfortunately, she wasn't able to stop the sudden closing of the window, the wind rattling the glass within its wooden casement. With a loud bang, it slammed shut.

Making her way across the last few feet, she stood in front of the closed window. Pressing her hands flat against the pane of glass, she pushed upwards. *Nothing.* The window refused to budge. Using her fingertips, she wedged them between the two sides of the frame and tried again. *Nothing.*

"Oh great, Jessi. Nine-thirty at night and you're locked out." Glancing down, she shook her head. "In your pajamas, no less. What else could possibly go wrong today?"

True to *Murphy's Law,* the wind picked up again, bringing with it a light spattering of rain. Huddling next to the window, Jessi did her best to stay beneath the gabled roof that peaked above her head.

Thunder rumbled off in the distance, causing her to weigh her options a little more quickly than she'd planned. She could work her way back to the tree and try climbing down that way. Pushing her hair back from her face, she studied the most obvious route.

The outstretched limb was narrow. If it broke, she'd fall and take the nest with her. While she would most likely survive the fall, the tiny birds wouldn't. Immediately, she discarded her first option.

The drain pipe was another possibility. Inching her way to the edge of the roof, Jessi lay on her belly and made her inspection by the light of the moon. Like the rest of the house, the pipe was well worn. With a trembling hand, she reached for the aluminum drain, only to have it detach itself from the

gutter and fall into the yard below. So much for option number
two.

Staring in disbelief at the damage she'd done, she shook
herself alert and began shouting at the top of her lungs,
demanding that someone come to her aid. Her voice was hoarse
before she realized the futility of her efforts. Nearly everywhere
she looked, the lights were off. Her neighbors were out and
about, rather than home baking cookies. The only lights that
burned were Mrs. McCurdy's, and she was half a block away
and stone deaf. Choice number three turned out to be as impossi-
ble as the first two.

Cautiously, Jessi made her way back to the center of the
roof. Settled beneath the overhang, she closed her eyes and
tried to think. Rather than solutions, came recriminations. "Oh,
Jessi, do you realize what you've done? For the personal satisfaction of saving one little bird, you've consigned yourself to
possibly an entire night on the roof."

The wind picked up, along with the rain, the twin assaults
sending a shiver through her and setting her teeth to chattering.
It felt as if the temperature had dropped ten degrees in the last
few minutes. Wrapping her arms around her legs, she laid her
forehead against her knees.

Immediately, the worst possible scenario came to mind. "Oh,
Jessi, what if you catch your death of cold?" she asked aloud.

She sighed deeply and blinked back unwanted tears. "You're
too young to die, Jessi. Heck—you haven't even lived yet. Just
think," she said, her voice firm with anger at herself and her
carelessness. "If you die, you'll never get the chance to see
the places you only glimpsed before. You'll never get to actually
see New York, or realize your dreams."

Dane stripped out of his uniform and donned his track shorts
and running shoes. Half-way through the door, he pulled a thin,
cotton t-shirt over his head. The need to run off some of his
tension had him taking the porch steps two at a time, his feet
hitting the rain-drenched pavement with a splash.

At the intersection he made his choice. Legs pumping, heart

pounding, he turned left, sparing only a quick, backward glance for his usual route. Most often he went to the right, through the small town square, across the public gardens, and past his office. The roads in that direction were familiar. *Safe.*

He didn't want familiar. He didn't want safe. He craved something more. He wanted different. As different as the red-haired pixy who had invaded his thoughts constantly since they'd met. He told himself he hadn't chosen the road to the left because of her, but because he needed a change. The fact that the less used route took him right past the Patterson's was merely a coincidence.

Liar!, his ever-present and well-used conscience taunted.

He turned right at Highgait Lane. The closer he came to Elmwood Avenue, the faster his pulse raced, the harder his heart pounded, the higher his legs pumped. Adrenalin flowed through him at an alarming rate, making him dizzy, yet powerful at the same time.

Turning the last corner, he saw the Patterson's house off in the distance. The downstairs lights were out. The upstairs apartment was nearly as dark, except for one light that shone through what Dane knew to be the kitchen window. Slowing his pace, he turned into the driveway, intending to do nothing more than circle around the yard and head back home.

That was when he heard the singing. Soft, lilting notes, interrupted by breathless gasps for air. Stopping beside the porch, he lifted his head and waited for the sound to come again.

Old Beatles tunes. *Hey Jude* mixed with *The Long and Winding Road,* both slightly off-key renditions reminding him of his happy-go-lucky youth. The singing ended abruptly, the final notes followed by a hiccup and a sneeze.

"Hello?" he called out. "Who's up there?"

"It's me," a raspy voice called, "Jessi. I'm stuck out here on the roof."

Dane heard the distant sound of shuffling feet. A moment later, Jessi was looking down at him from the edge of the roof.

"Oh wonderful," she said excitedly, "the cavalry's arrived. I'm saved."

Shaking his head in disbelief, he asked, "Is the door open?"

"No. I locked it. Now what will we do?"

"Hold on a minute, Miss Trainor," he assured her. "I'll be right back."

The first thing he noticed was the fallen drain pipe. Thank goodness she'd not been on it when it fell. He checked the garage for a ladder. There was none. Next, he checked the door leading to the apartment. The lock was sturdy, as was the frame. The window pane was sectioned into six squares. Taking off his t-shirt, he wrapped it around his hand. With one solid tap, the window broke, the glass splintering and the ragged shards falling to the floor.

Within seconds he had the door unlocked and open. He crossed the kitchen in three long strides and reached for the window. The flip-latch had fallen into place and, after lifting it, he eased the window upward.

"Miss Trainor?" he called.

"Right here, sheriff," she acknowledged, poking her head through the window.

Work-roughened, yet gentle, hands dragged her inside and held her upright when she would have fallen.

"Are you all right?" he asked.

His concern was evident by the soothing tone of his deeply masculine voice. Despite the emotional warmth his words provided, Jessi shivered. "Yes . . . I'm . . . fine." Her teeth chattering, she stumbled over her response.

"No you're not," he contradicted, "you're freezing. Where do you keep your blankets?"

"In . . . the . . . bedroom . . . closet."

"Wait here," he said, seating her in a nearby chair. "I'll be right back."

Jessi stared after him, his long legs quickly eating up the distance between the kitchen and her bedroom. Within seconds he was back, the quilt from her bed clutched tightly in his grasp.

"You need to get out of those wet pajamas."

Jessi glanced down at her soaking wet frame. The red silk pajamas hugged her body like a second skin . . . a tight glove.

What few curves she had stood out in intimate relief beneath the wet material. Self-consciously, she wrapped her arms around her middle and sniffled.

Dane pulled her from the chair, steering her toward the small bathroom. Pushing her inside, he asked, "Can you manage on your own?"

"Yes . . . I . . . can . . . thank . . . you."

"I'll be waiting right here. Call out if you need help."

Jessi shut the door between them, her chilled hands fumbling with the hook-and-eye lock. *Call out if you need help. Right.*

"You should take a hot shower," he suggested through the door. "If you'd like, I'll make a pot of tea."

"Thank . . . you. Tea would be nice." She sneezed.

"Bless you."

"Th . . . an . . . ks," she managed before sneezing once more.

Hands trembling, she stripped out of her wet clothes, and turned on the shower. The distant sound of Sheriff Logan moving around her kitchen drew her attention and her smile. She'd never had a man make tea for her before. Come to think of it, she'd never had a man in her apartment before. The idea drew a second, stronger, tremble that had nothing to do with being cold.

Dane set the tea kettle on the stove and searched the cupboards for cups. In the cabinet over the refrigerator he found a bottle of cooking sherry. He took it down and added a healthy shot to Jessi's mug. While he waited for the water to boil, he gathered the pieces of broken glass and put them in the garbage. All the time he worked, he thought of how lucky Jessi had been that he'd come by. Things could have been worse. Much worse.

The shower stopped running, and he called out, "Are you okay in there?"

"Yes." she called back. "I'm fine now."

Dane closed his eyes and breathed a sigh of relief. Immediately, Jessi's vision invaded the dark recesses of his mind. With vivid clarity, he remembered how she'd looked in her soaking wet pajamas, her hair hanging limply across her shoulders, her eyes wide with a mixture of fear and embarrassment, her small curves apparent . . .

His eyes snapped open, his gaze focusing on the tea kettle, its shrill whistle drawing him back to reality with a jolt. Shutting off the stove, he lifted the kettle and poured steaming water into a china teapot. He'd no sooner reached the table with cups and pot in hand, when Jessi emerged from the bathroom.

She'd foregone the bedding for a heavy terrycloth bathrobe that hung to her ankles. She held the patchwork quilt in front of her like a shield. She'd brushed her hair and tied the loose ends back with a piece of ribbon. Her cheeks were flushed with heat and her eyes were glassy.

"Okay?" he asked.

"Kinda. Although, I'm a bit embarrassed about being so careless and locking myself out on the roof."

Watching her from behind the steam that rose from his mug of tea, he grinned. "How did you happen to be out there?"

Jessi stared out through the window, searching in the dark for an excuse that wouldn't sound ridiculous. Only the truth seemed right. "I was saving a baby bird who had fallen from his nest. I didn't realize the window would close, otherwise I would have used something to prop it open."

"How long were you out there?"

She glanced at the clock, her eyes widening in amazement at what she saw. "Ohmygosh . . . it's after eleven."

"How long?"

The seriousness in his voice drew Jessi's gaze from the clock to the man. Their gazes met and, as they had done in his office, meshed. He smiled and her heart fluttered, the infinite tremble sending a wave of warmth through her body.

"Two hours, give or take a few minutes," she said finally.

His expression changed suddenly, the smile that had warmed her only moments before, turning into a frown. She'd seen that reaction before. She knew what it meant. *Disappointment.*

It hadn't taken long for the handsome sheriff to form an opinion. Like her parents, her ex-coach, and two previous employers, Dane Logan obviously saw her for what she was . . . an inept failure.

"Listen," she said suddenly, "I'm fine now. I don't want to detain you any longer."

"It's no problem, I—"

"I'd like to go to bed, if you don't mind."

He nodded. In one lithe movement, he pushed the chair back and stood. Within two strides, he'd reached the door.

"I'll come by tomorrow and fix this broken window," he told her.

"That won't—"

"I insist," he interrupted. "I broke it, I'll fix it. And, I'll get someone to repair the drain pipe."

She nodded. "Okay. Thank you."

Fine. I know when I'm not wanted.

You should be grateful, Jessi Trainor, that I came along. If I hadn't shown up, you might have frozen to death. Or—at the least—caught one helluva cold.

Dane's thoughts egged him on, his anger pushing him faster and faster until he'd covered the three-quarter mile distance between Jessi Trainor's apartment and his own house in less than three minutes. The rain, falling harder than before, drenched him clear through to the bone.

Standing on the wide front porch, he drew in deep drafts of air. Pressing his fingertips to his wrist he measured his pulse. Damn the woman anyway! Crazy child didn't know when to come in out of the rain!

You don't mean that.

"Yes, I do," he mumbled to himself.

Child. The label echoed through his thoughts, confirming for him the problem he was having with this sudden attraction. So young.

Ten years isn't such a big difference.

So innocent, and I'm anything but. The differences in that respect can't be measured in years.

So, you'll adjust. Something tells me, Jessi Trainor's worth the effort. What've you got to lose?

My sanity for one thing.

Hell, Logan, you lost that years ago.

The teasing of his conscience did nothing to improve his dark mood. Women were nothing but trouble—with a capital T. Unlocking the front door, he stepped inside. The house was dark and cool. And empty. A chill ran through him, reminding him he was wet, and cold, and hungry. The cold and wet he could easily remedy with a hot shower. The hunger was another matter.

Somehow he doubted food would do the trick.

Two

Jessi's head hurt and she had a mild fever, both compliments of her sojourn on the roof. Common sense told her that she owed Sheriff Logan an apology for her abrupt behavior of the night before—a fact that only added to the pounding of her head and the flush of her cheeks.

Jessi acknowledged that she also owed Dane Logan a debt of gratitude. Had he not come along when he did, she might well be in the hospital. Instead, she was destined for a stuffy nose and aching head, both of which she readily deserved. Not for the first time—or the last—would she dispute her ineptness; her penchant for getting into ridiculous situations.

Face it, Trainor, you're a screw-up; a failure.

As badly as she wanted to refute her conscience's claim, the facts were clear. When she should have been strong, she'd crumbled. When people had counted on her, she'd let them down.

Jessi closed her eyes and inhaled the pungent aroma of the apple muffins she'd just removed from the oven. The cinnamon-scented air permeated every one of her five senses, relaxing her, reminding her of all she'd accomplished. All her successes. The faint voice of her self-worth spoke up at last, contradicting her conscience's claims on her behalf.

You're not a failure, Jessi. Your cookbooks are best sellers.
You have an exciting career. Forget the past. It's not important.

A light tap at the kitchen door drew Jessi back to reality;
back to the possibility of failure.

No, Jessi. Success.

On the opposite side of the screen door stood Dane Logan.
In his hands he held a rectangular section of glass, a putty
knife, and a tube of sealant. Although his sky-blue eyes were
hidden behind a pair of dark glasses, his smile was warm and
friendly. Dressed in his starched brown uniform, his wheat-
gold hair ruffled haphazardly by the lightweight breeze, he
looked fantastic.

"Good morning, Miss Trainor."

"Good morning, Sheriff." After a moment's hesitation, she
added, "Please, call me Jessi."

"Okay . . . Jessi, but only if you'll call me Dane."

Jessi nodded, then backed up and let him in. Her compact
kitchen seemed to shrink even more when he crossed the thresh-
old and stepped into the room. Surprisingly, Jessi found herself
at a loss for words—a feeling quite new for her, and very
unsettling.

"Coffee?" she asked, finally finding her tongue.

"Yes, please."

While she poured two cups of coffee, Dane spread out the
items needed to repair the broken window.

"Cream? Sugar?"

"No thank you. Black is fine."

"Muffin? They're hot from the oven."

"You cook quite a bit, don't you?"

"It comes with the job. I test every recipe three times before
I put it in my cookbook. I also use recipes other people give
me and experiment with various changes. Fresh ingredients
that are abundant in Michigan might not be readily available
in Arizona. My cookbooks have to be universal."

He seemed to be assessing her with his eyes, his gaze creating
an unaccustomed tingle on the surface of her skin. Drawing a
breath to still the flutter of her heartbeat, Jessi met his gaze.
His slow smile set a stronger rhythm beating within her breast.

"Obviously, you don't eat everything you cook."

"No, but I do taste everything. Then, most often, I give the food away. As a matter of fact, I'll be delivering my muffins and the four dozen cookies I baked yesterday to the residents of Oak Manor. They're always grateful for my leftovers."

"No doubt. I imagine retirement home food can be pretty bland. Your generosity is very commendable."

His compliment sifted through her like a warm rain, and she smiled and asked, "Well, do you want one, or not?"

"Sure."

Dane set his tools aside and joined Jessi at the formica-topped table. The coffee smelled delicious—not at all like the mud Deputy Pike made. The muffins, big and bursting with chunks of apples, looked far better than the greasy eggs and burnt toast he'd had before leaving home. His hostess, dressed in tight jeans and baggy sweatshirt, looked as delicious as the food she set before him.

Around a bite of warm muffin, he mumbled, "mmm . . ." After he'd swallowed both the muffin and a mouthful of steaming coffee, he complimented, "delicious."

Seeing the light that sparkled in Jessi's eyes, he took another bite and a second drink. What he really wanted, he realized, was a tasty nibble of the smooth skin at her throat and a sip of her smile. Instead, he settled for what she offered. A muffin and coffee.

It hadn't taken Dane long to fix the window pane. In less than twenty minutes, he'd finished his coffee, completed the repairs, and took his leave. It was almost as if he couldn't wait to get away. When she'd offered him her hand in thanks, he'd grasped it lightly and pulled away so fast that she'd barely felt the heat of his palm. Had it not been for the distinct, yet fleeting, current of electricity passing between his hand and hers, she'd have almost thought she'd offended him. Then, he'd left so quickly, she hadn't had the opportunity to apologize for her abrupt behavior the night before. Or, to thank him a second time for coming to her rescue.

Jessi packed her basket with the muffins, cookies, and a batch of fudge she'd made right after Dane had left. As with the cookies she had baked the night before, the solace she usually found in cooking did little toward easing her jangled nerves where Dane Logan was concerned.

She definitely needed to find another form of mental diversion.

Just as Jessi'd known they would, the residents of Oak Manor were more than willing to partake in her bountiful basket. While the kitchen staff brewed tea and coffee, Jessi and her friend Karen Seils set out the cookies, muffins, and fudge. Karen had been the one to invite her to Brant Mills; the one to encourage her when others had shown only their disappointment.

"You're a very special person, Jessi. The residents love your twice-weekly visits."

"There's nothing special about donating leftover test recipes, Kar. Special is being here for these people day in and day out. It's you and your staff who are special. I envy your strength and decisiveness. You never make mistakes."

Although Karen looked as if she wanted to refute Jessi's claim, she held her tongue and smiled sweetly. "Thank you, Jessi. You always add a huge ray of sunshine to my day." After only a moment's hesitation, she added, "Maybe someday, Jessi Trainor, you'll shower some of that sunshine on yourself and quit putting yourself down."

It was an old argument between old friends, and Jessi knew better than to disagree. Rather than reply, she shrugged her shoulders and turned away. Disguising the emotion in her voice behind a curtain of stern reprimand, she scolded, "Mr. Rollins. I saw you sneak that cookie."

By the time the treats had been served, the dishes collected and delivered to the kitchen, Jessi had almost convinced herself that she could—at times—do something right. Something useful.

Evelyn Trumble, the home's eldest citizen, was asleep in a nearby chair. Mr. Rollins, Jessi's undisputed favorite, sat off to one side with his newspaper. One and all, these people accepted her. They liked her. And, as always, they regaled her with praise for her culinary efforts. Jessi left Oak Manor feeling quite pleased with herself, and with life in general.

The day had turned warm and sunny. The walk from Oak Manor to her apartment, although nearly two miles long, was a pleasant one. The most direct route took her through the heart of town, past the handful of businesses. Right past the sheriff's office.

Deputy Pike sat in a large, barrel-shaped chair in front of the office, his foot propped against the railing. When Jessi was within earshot, he looked up and grinned, his bushy mustache twitching as he asked, "Seen any flashers lately, Ma'am?"

Jessi shook her head, her gaze clashing with Deputy Pike's. The memory of having to repeat her story over and over again had her rushing her steps. She'd barely passed where Pike sat when a second voice hailed her from behind.

"Jessi?"

She stopped and turned around slowly. Dane's gentle smile was a direct and welcome counterpoint to the grin on Pike's face.

"Yes, Sheriff Logan?"

The sudden twitch of his lips reminded her of his edict that she call him Dane. His short nod of acknowledgement told her that he realized she preferred using his title in front of his deputy.

"How'd things go at the Manor?" Dane asked.

"Fine. All the food disappeared."

"Food?" Pike exclaimed.

"Yeah, Pike," Dane explained, "Jessi writes cookbooks. When she tests recipes, she takes the leftovers to Oak Manor."

"What kind of leftovers?"

"Today it was cookies and muffins," Jessi told him, "and fudge."

The deputy swallowed, his interest piqued. "Fudge?"

"Yes. Chocolate fudge."

"Maybe," Dane hastened to point out, "if you and the boys

would of been a little nicer to Miss Trainor, she might have offered you a leftover or two.''

"We were only funnin', Dane. You know that."

"An apology might go a long way toward garnering a taste or two."

Dane's suggestion drew, what Jessi thought to be, Pike's most sincere smile. "Me and the boys were only teasing, Miss Trainor. I'm sorry if we upset you."

"Apology accepted, Mr. Pike. I'll be working on a recipe this evening. If you and the other deputies would consider being my guinea pigs, I'll deliver the results of my efforts first thing tomorrow morning."

"We'd be right honored, Miss Trainor," Pike assured her.

"Fine, then. I'll see you both in the morning. Around ten."

Pike doffed his hat. "Sure thing, Ma'am. We'll be here."

Jessi moved on down the street, stopping in front of Larson's Drugs and Molly McQuaide's bookstore. Her attention drawn to Miss McQuaide's colorful display, she started when Dane spoke.

"You've captured Pike's rusty old heart, Jessi."

Pressing a hand to her own rapidly beating heart, she lifted her gaze. "Sher. . . . Dane . . . you startled me."

"I'm sorry. I thought you knew I'd followed you."

"No. I thought I was alone."

Dane shrugged his broad shoulders and diverted his gaze to the display in the window. Jessi's gaze followed.

After a very pronounced silence, Jessi told him, "I have to go. I need supplies for tonight's baking."

"Were you really testing recipes tonight?"

"Tonight, tomorrow night. There's not much difference."

Dane grinned, his eyes twinkling with mirth. "You'll have my deputies wrapped around your little finger with the very first taste. Try not to take advantage of them."

"I'd never—" she stammered, appalled that he'd think . . .

"I'm just teasing, Jessi."

She tried looking stern, but knew she'd failed miserably when he grinned and added, "You're easy to tease, Jessi

Trainor. Every change of emotion shows like a bright red flag on your beautifully flawless skin.''

Beautifully flawless skin?

"If you'll excuse me, Sheriff, the store closes early today." With her hastily given excuses, she hurried down the sidewalk, away from Dane Logan and his silver tongue and sensual teasing.

Sheriff? He'd been demoted. And all because he'd offered her a compliment. Obviously, his teasing made her nervous. It made him nervous, too. And restless. If he had half a brain in his head, he'd stay away from Jessi Trainor. Before he did something really rash. Like asking her out on a date. Or worse yet, like stroking those flame-colored cheeks with his fingertips and kissing those delectable cherry lips.

With a shake of his head, he acknowledged that her hasty retreat was exactly what he deserved, especially considering the way he'd fled her apartment earlier that morning. He'd certainly been restless then. With Jessi Trainor around, restlessness was a condition he was quickly learning to accept.

Jessi, her arms laden with groceries, rounded the corner of Elm and Highgait. One more block and she'd be home. She'd be safe. And alone.

Mrs. McCurdy was out on her porch tending her begonias. She lifted a hand in greeting.

"Hi," Jessi called, even though she knew the elderly woman couldn't hear her.

Halfway down the street, Jessi called out to Mary Taylor. "Morning, Mary."

"Oh, Jessi," the visibly pregnant Mary called. "Am I glad to see you."

At the sight of Mary holding tightly to her huge belly, Jessi hastened forward, setting her bags down on Mary's porch. "What's the matter, Mary."

"I'm in labor. Hard labor," she gasped. "I tried reaching Kevin on his car phone, but he didn't answer. Finally, I left a message with his answering service."

"Did you call your doctor?" Jessi asked.

"Yes. He said to get to the hospital as soon as possible, but I'm in no condition to drive. I tried calling an ambulance, but there are only two in this area, and they were both out on emergencies. I guess everyone's getting sick at once."

"I can take you," Jessi offered.

"I couldn't ask you to do that, Jessi. The hospital's nearly thirty miles away."

"It's no trouble, if you don't mind me driving your car."

Mary shook her head. "No problem. Just let me call the hospital and tell them we're on the way. Could you get my bag from the hallway and put it in the car?"

"Sure," Jessi agreed. "I'll just set my groceries inside the house."

Jessi settled in behind the wheel of the Taylor's big station wagon. "Okay," she stated firmly, getting a grip on her nervousness and, hopefully, reassuring Mary at the same time. "We're off."

Jessi pulled the car out onto Elmwood, turning left toward highway eight. Mary, pale as a ghost, was busy with her breathing exercises and timing the frequency of her contractions.

"Don't worry, Mary, I'll have you to the hospital in no time."

The pavement was shiny black from the late afternoon humidity. The illusion of heat rose up in the air, creating a mesmerizing mirage. Fifteen miles out of town, the car started to choke and sputter. As they slowed to a complete halt, Jessi stared at the dashboard. With a shake of her head, she accepted the inevitable. They were out of gas.

"Oh . . . shoot!"

Frantically, Mary asked, "What is it, Jessi?"

"We're out of gas."

"We can't be. Kevin always keeps the car filled. He always . . ." Her voice trailed away on another wave of pain; another strong contraction.

Well, Jessi, what are you going to do now?

Shut up! she warned her taunting conscience.

Mary gripped the dashboard and panted her way through the end of her contraction.

"How far apart are the pains?" Jessi asked. Although she wasn't sure what difference that made, given the circumstances, it was the first question that came to mind.

"Four and half minutes—sometimes less."

"Someone's sure to come by. I'd better put the hood up."

"Yes," Mary agreed. "Highway ten is always busy."

Jessi didn't like admitting that she'd taken the less used, shorter route, but she felt Mary had the right to know.

"We're not on ten. We're on eight."

"Eight? Oh, Jessi, nobody ever comes down eight."

Jessi bit hard into her lower lip to stifle the urge to cry. One look at Mary, consumed by another round of pain, and the tears she'd tried so hard to squelch slipped freely down her cheeks.

"I'm sorry, Mary," Jessi whispered. "So very sorry."

"Oh . . . god . . . Jessi. It's not your fault," Mary cried.

Mary's absolution did nothing to ease Jessi's conscience.

"What will we do, Jessi?"

Jessi closed her eyes and drew a deep breath, willing her heart to stop pounding and her hands to stop shaking. In the strongest voice she could muster, Jessi told her, "We'll do what we have to, Mary. I won't let you down, I promise."

I won't let you down. I promise. Jessi's own words echoed in her ears. *Oh, Mary, what have I done?*

Three

Dane turned his patrol car onto the side street leading past the Taylor's two-story bungalow, his promise to Kevin Taylor ringing loudly in his ears. In a panic, the father-to-be had called from the hospital in Milton, and Dane had promised to cover all possible routes between Brant Mills and Milton in search of Mary Taylor.

Kevin assured him he'd criss-crossed all of highway ten and most of the short feeder routes. That left highway eight. Dane turned left at Highgate and drove out of town.

Off in the distance, the late afternoon sun seemed to teeter on the horizon, suspended between daylight and dusk. The temperature, in the low eighties all day, now registered a comfortable seventy-two. Crossing the fine line between town and country, Dane pushed the accelerator closer to the floor.

"Where are you, Mary?" Dane wondered aloud. "Why would you even think of driving yourself to Milton?"

Kevin's greatest worry had been Mary's driving while in labor. He'd also expressed concern that he hadn't put gas in the car in ages. "I hadn't expected her to drive," he'd said, "especially not in the throes of labor."

Flicking on the emergency lights, Dane increased his speed to just short of ninety-five.

"It's okay, Mary," Jessi rushed to reassure, "I know everything's going to work out. Let's get you into the back of the station wagon where you can be comfortable."

Mary gritted her teeth and let out a low, rumbling, cry. Jessi glanced down at her watch, just as she had less than two minutes earlier.

"Jessi," Mary gasped, "we're going to have to do this ourselves. Once you've spread out the blanket, you can help me get out of these slacks."

Jessi's hands trembled where she clutched the huge red and green plaid blanket. Yet, for the life of her, she wouldn't dare let Mary see her fear. "Okay, the blanket's ready. Let me help you up."

Mary had no sooner scooted into the back of the station wagon when Jessi saw the flash of the rotating red and white lights. "Oh, Mary. Look!"

"What is it, Jessi?" Mary whispered, her hands clenched against a strong contraction.

"It looks like an ambulance, or a fire rescue truck. Everything's going to be all right, just like I said."

The closer the emergency vehicle came, the easier Jessi found it to breath, the less frantically her heart beat. By the time the brown and white, and very familiar, car screeched to a halt beside the station wagon, Jessi was in no doubt as to who their savior was.

"It's Dane," Jessi confirmed for her friend. "He's going to get us to the hospital after all."

Just as Dane reached the back of the car, Mary screamed out in pain. "No . . . he's . . . not . . ." she cried, ". . . the . . . baby's . . . coming. Now."

Dane met Jessi's gaze for less than a second before he turned away, but not before she saw his disappointment. Most likely, he held her responsible for the danger Mary faced. Most likely, she conceded, he was right.

Dane laid a firm, reassuring hand on Mary's belly. "How's it going, Mary?"

"Just great," she managed on a half-laugh, half-cry. "I'm afraid we don't have time to . . ." Her words halted on another contraction. Her fingers closed tightly around Jessi's offered hand.

"Don't worry, Mary," Dane said softly—confidently. "I've delivered more babies than I care to count."

In uncanny unison, Jessi and Mary asked, "You have?"

"Sure."

"What can I do to help?" Jessi asked.

"Right now, I need you to help Mary through the next few contractions. Make sure she practices her breathing and doesn't push. I've gotta call this in and grab the first aid kit. I'll be back before you know it."

"Don't worry," Jessi shakily told him, "we're not going anywhere."

As promised, Dane was back within minutes, his arms laden down with a spare blanket, a large first aid kit, and a folding stand like the type waiters used to hold trays of food. With a flick of his wrists, he set up the stand and laid the kit on top.

"Here," he instructed, handing the extra blanket to Jessi, "use this to bolster her up a bit."

From inside the first aid kit, he withdrew the needed supplies, along with two neatly folded paper sheets. "Help Mary out of the last of her things from the waist down, then drape one of these over her knees."

Jessi knew she should have been embarrassed, both for herself and for Mary, but the gravity of the situation erased all restrictive emotion from her thoughts.

Methodically, Dane washed his hands with bottled soap and water, rising them in an alcohol solution. Slipping into a thin pair of sterile rubber gloves, he lifted the sheet draped across Mary's knees and took his first look at the task before him.

Absently, he wondered if two babies constituted *more than he cared to count.*

"Well," he confirmed, "you were right. There's not much

time. The ambulance is on the way, but it's doubtful this little bundle's gonna wait.''

Jessi, he realized, was beside him, still as a statue and twice as white as the finest Italian marble. "You okay?"

"Yeah, sure," Jessi mumbled.

"Oooo. . . . Dane. . . . please. . . ." Mary gasped, her hands gripping the blanket beneath her for leverage.

"It's okay, Mary, we're right here."

"We?" Jessi asked nervously. "I don't—"

"Look," Dane interrupted, "there's the head."

Pressing a hand to her gaping mouth, Jessi exclaimed, "Oh . . . my . . ."

"Don't faint on me Trainor. I'm gonna need some help here."

Jessi doubted she'd be around for actual delivery. Her knees were knocking so loudly, and her heart racing so fast, she would surely hit the pavement long before the baby presented itself.

"What do you want me to do?" she asked, suprised by the sudden surge of strength she felt welling up from within.

"First off, use some of that water to soak one of those washcloths. Wipe off Mary's face and wet her lips. Then, get a pair of gloves on and spread out that other sheet. We'll wrap the baby in it as soon as I've cut the cord."

Jessi followed Dane's orders to the letter, all the while cooing non-sensical phrases to Mary and her unborn child.

"Okay," Dane instructed, "it's time to bear down, Mary. Take a deep breath and push."

It was the most remarkable thing Jessi had ever witnessed. Despite the obvious pain, Mary breathed and pushed and breathed and pushed. Dane continued offering words of encouragement and instruction. Jessi followed Dane's nods and motions and rushed orders. On the six or seventh push, the baby's head came, followed by the slim shoulders and slippery body. The perfectly formed legs and feet—with five perfect toes each—followed suit.

"Oh, Dane," Jessi whispered in awe, "it's a girl. A beautiful girl."

Dane motioned for the rubber suction bulb, quickly clearing

the baby's nose and mouth. His careful ministrations elicited the first gurgles, followed by a lusty howl and the cries Jessi had held her breath waiting to hear.

"A beautiful baby girl," Dane agreed.

Tears ran freely down Mary's cheeks. "Really?"

"Yes," he assured her. "Really."

Jessi took the baby from Dane's hands and laid her on Mary's stomach while Dane clamped and cut the cord. Using the damp cloth she'd prepared, she wiped the baby's face. At Dane's nod, she wrapped the baby in the paper sheet and laid her in her mother's anxiously reaching arms.

"Oh look, Jessi," Mary sobbed happily, "she is perfect. Aren't you, Jessica?"

"Jessica?" Jessi repeated.

"Of course. I couldn't very well call her Dane, could I?"

"No, I—"

The distant wail of the arriving ambulance saved Jessi from making a blubbering fool of herself. While they waited, Jessi busied herself with the task of cleaning up the mess the impromptu delivery had created.

"You did good, Jessi."

Dane's praise filtered through Jessi like a wonderfully healing balm. She'd been watching the efficient paramedics load Mary and baby Jessica into the waiting ambulance, thinking about how wonderful Dane had been, and worrying over the reprimand that was sure to come, when he'd come up behind her. Resigned to the fact that she'd screwed up once more, she waited for his admonishment.

You did good, Jessi. There was nothing he could have said that would have surprised her more.

"It was all my fault," she said. Why she felt compelled to point that fact out was beyond her. She should have left well enough alone.

"I'm sure Mary won't fault you for any of this."

"No, of course not. In the excitement of the moment, neither of us thought about the gas gage.'' Turning to face him, she lifted her head and met his gaze. "Still, I should have been—''

"Shh," he told her, cutting off her recriminations with the tip of one finger. "Don't. Everything's fine. There's no need badgering yourself with what might have been.''

"I suppose you're right," she admitted willingly.

"Of course I'm right. I'm the sheriff. I'm always right.'' His teasing banter lifted the weight she'd let settle on her shoulders.

"What about Mary's car?''

"Deputy Pike is on his way with gas. He and Stevens will see that it gets back to town.''

"I could drive. I—''

"I'm driving you home," he insisted. "Right after we go by the hospital and check on the new father.''

Jessi had only met Kevin Taylor once. He was a big man, she noted now. Yet, he seemed so fragile at the moment. So vulnerable. Sitting at his wife's side, he held her hand. Mary was asleep.

"We owe you both a debt of thanks," Kevin said softly. "If Mary had been alone, I hate to think what might have happened.''

Jessi was about to dispute her part in the drama when Dane's hand closed tightly around hers, a silent communication between the two of them.

"For someone who's never been exposed to childbirth, Jessi did an admirable job as my assistant.''

"I imagine," Kevin pointed out, "when she wakes up from all this, Mary's going to be a little embarrassed.''

"No," Jessi disagreed, "she shouldn't be. Giving birth is the most wonderful thing a woman can do. If she mentions one word about embarrassment, you set her straight. What happened out there on the highway was an honest-to-goodness miracle, and nothing to be embarrassed over.''

For all her bravado, Jessi still felt the warm flush coating her cheeks. She still remembered Dane's praise. *You did good,*

Jessi. The thought of pleasing him sent a second, warmer flush to her skin.

Every emotion shows vividly on your flawless skin. The memory of Dane's words drew her smile.

Within the half-hour, Dane and Jessi were on their way back to Brant Mills. Jessi sat in the front seat of the patrol car, her side pressed firmly to the door, as if she couldn't get far enough away from him.

"I'm not going to bite, you know," he told her.

"I know that. I guess I'm the one who's embarrassed now. I can't believe what we . . . what *you* did. It was so amazing."

"You played as important a part as I did, Jessi. I couldn't have done it without you."

She shook her head in denial. "You would have if you'd had to. You're always in control."

No I'm not. There's no control to be had around you, Jessi.

"I appreciate your confidence, Jessi. But, truth be told, I was scared to death. I was just too busy to let it show."

"But why? You knew exactly what you were doing. Like you said, you'd delivered so many—"

"Three," he admitted. "And that's including baby Jessica."

"Three?" she repeated.

"Yeah, three."

Jessi giggled once . . . twice . . . the infectious sound coating his heart and soul with warmth.

Wiping tears from the corners of her eyes, she teased, "You've obviously missed your calling in life."

"What? You think I'd have made a good doctor?"

The thought made her laugh all the harder. A hiccup interrupted her first attempt at speaking.

"No," she finally managed, "but you'd have made one heck of a poker player."

Darkness settled in around them, enclosing Dane and his passenger in a comfortable cloak of gray. On the opposite side of the patrol car, Jessi was fast asleep, her hands tucked up beneath her cheek and resting on the back of the seat. The urge to reach out and pull her toward him had him clutching the steering wheel so hard that his knuckles were white.

You don't need this, his inner-voice told him.

Yes, I do, he argued. *I need this very much.*

He wasn't sure how this one particular woman-child had gotten to him so fast, but she had, and there was no help for it. In the back of his overworked mind, he realized he would have to tread carefully where Jessi Trainor was concerned.

He'd bet everything he owned that she was as innocent as they came. He'd also bet that, with no more than a touch, she could set him on fire. The two equations didn't fit.

Jessi, he also realized, had a problem with self-esteem. She'd obviously led a somewhat sheltered life, and had probably been on her own for a very short time. He wondered about her past, and what had caused her deflated opinion of herself, and her habit of continuously apologizing for things beyond her control. He also wondered how she happened to get herself into the most unusual situations.

The thought of being Jessi's knight in shining armor brought a smile to his lips. Yeah, he admitted silently, being Jessi's hero would be the perfect part time job.

Jessi wiped the residue of sleep from her eyes. Blinking, she acclimated herself to her surroundings. She was in the patrol car. Dane sat behind the wheel, yet the car wasn't moving. They were parked.

Half-asleep, she stared out into the darkness, doing her best to identify her surroundings. The Patterson's driveway. They were in the Patterson's driveway.

"Oh, we've arrived."

"About twenty minutes ago." Dane's voice, she noted, was low and husky and sexy. And, the most exciting thing she'd ever heard.

"But—"

"I didn't want to wake you," he said simply. "Obviously, you were beat."

"But—"

"Besides," he interrupted a second time, "I like watching you sleep."

"You do?"

"Yes, I do."

"Oh." Reaching for the door handle, she told him, "I'd better be going. I—"

The first touch of Dane's fingertips against her cheek stilled her words and shot a current of electricity through her right down to the very soles of her feet. Even her toes tingled.

"Jessi," he murmured softly. "Where did you come from, Jessi Trainor? Why are you here?"

She opened her mouth to answer, yet nothing came out. From somewhere deep inside, she realized his question was rhetorical.

The feather-like touch of his fingers slid from her cheek to her lips. Using the pad of his thumb, he stroked her lower lip. Softly. Slowly. Until Jessi thought she might faint from his gentle caress. Despite the warmth of his touch, she trembled.

"Dane?" she questioned. Had that thick, husky, sound come from her?

"If you promise not to slap me, I think I'd like to kiss you."

"I won't slap you. I promise."

He leaned forward, his lips hovering a scant few inches above hers. *Well, Jessi, this is what you wanted. Isn't it?* "Yes," she whispered, the fact that she'd answered her conscience's question aloud dawning on her a heartbeat later when Dane answered in kind.

"Yes," he echoed.

The first touch of his lips to hers set off the most beautiful skyrockets Jessi had ever seen, all wonderfully displayed behind her closed eyelids.

Don't blow this, Jessi. Whatever you do, don't show him how nervous you are. Or, how badly you want another kiss. You wouldn't want to appear greedy? Would you?

Jessi?"

Slowly, she opened her eyes. "Hmm . . ."

"You're home. It's time to wake up."

"*Wake up?* Jessi blinked her eyes, batting away the last remnants of sleep.

Wake up? Oh, dear Lord, she'd only dreamed Dane's kiss. It hadn't been real, no matter how wonderful it had been.

"Yes," she agreed. "I guess I'd better."

He stepped out of the car and walked to the opposite side. In those few seconds, Jessi composed herself. When Dane opened her door, she stepped out into the comfortable evening breeze.

"Thank you for the ride home."

"You're welcome, Jessi. Goodnight."

Jessi had barely reached the bottom step leading to her apartment, when Dane asked, "What about your groceries? Didn't you say you'd left your groceries at the Taylor's."

"Yes, I did. In all the excitement, I'd forgotten all about them."

"Kevin will be home tomorrow morning," he told her. "I'll go by and pick them up for you."

"That's not necessary," she told him, "I can get them myself."

"I don't mind. It'll give me an excuse to have another cup of your coffee."

"You like my coffee?"

"Very much so."

Hoping her heart wasn't beating loud enough to drown out her words, she asked, "How about breakfast? It's the least I can do to thank you for coming to my rescue . . . again."

"Jessi, you've got to stop—"

"Yes, or no," she interrupted. Immediately, she felt contrite for the sharpness of her tone of voice. She lifted her gaze to apologize and found him staring at her. His gaze drew hers, reeling her in, a willing captive to his sky-blue snare.

"Breakfast sounds great. What time?"

Right now. All night. First thing in the morning, right after our shower. Where had those totally unfamiliar, and thoroughly delicious, thoughts come from?

Rather than voice her newly-realized desires, she told him, "About nine. Will that give you time to retrieve my groceries?"

"Nine sounds great. I'll see you then."

Jessi checked her appearance for the hundredth time, her nervous pacing taking her from bedroom, to bathroom, to the window overlooking the driveway. Where was he?

She stopped in front of the kitchen clock, sparing a harsh glare for the fork and spoon hands that had the nerve to remind her that Dane was forty minutes late.

He's not coming.

"Shut up. What do you know?" she said aloud, calling her conscience out for a verbal skirmish.

I know he's not coming.

"He's been detained, that's all."

Or. he's changed his mind.

She was about to offer her rebuttal when a tap sounded at the kitchen door. Mustering up all the patience she possessed, she strolled nonchalantly toward the sound.

"Good morning, Dane," she greeted, her gaze affixed on his broad smile.

"Good morning, Jessi," he responded. "Sorry, I'm late." His arms were filled with her groceries, the cumbersome sight urging her to open the door.

"Come in, please. Let me take one of those."

"It's okay. I can manage. Just point me toward where you want me."

Down the hall, first door on the left. "Shh," she admonished herself.

"What did you say?"

"Ah . . . nothing."

"This okay here?"

"Yes, that's fine."

Dane set the bags down and backed away from the counter.

"I see the boys came by and fixed the drain pipe."

"Yes, remind me to thank them."

"They're eagerly awaiting payment by way of food. Both Pike and Stevens are widowers. Home cooking is a luxury they seldom get to enjoy."

"What about you, Dane? Do you get much home cooking?"

Oh great, Jessi! Why don't you just ask him about his sex life?

At least he didn't laugh his way to the door.

"Not much. About the only meal I've mastered is hot dogs and beans. And only if the beans come from a can."

Jessi breathed a sigh of relief, grateful that he hadn't taken offense to her poorly thought out question. "Have a seat while I fix breakfast."

"Mind if I pour myself a cup of coffee?"

"No, of course not. Help yourself."

Do you get much home cooking? Jessi's quest for information was less than subtle, but he didn't mind. Just the knowledge that she might be interested was enough to encourage him; enough to make him willing to tell her anything she wanted to know.

She moved around the kitchen with practiced ease. From counter, to cupboard, to sink, to refrigerator, each shift of her hips, each sway of her long, glorious mane of hair, sending shock waves through his system, settling warmly—uncomfortably—right where they had no business settling.

"Watcha making?" he asked. As a diversion it wasn't much, but the best he could do at the moment.

"Applesauce pancakes with hot honey sauce."

Dane licked his lips in anticipation. Belatedly, he thought of the pancakes. "Can I help?"

"I thought you didn't cook."

"I stir really well."

Not nearly as well as Jessi does. She's got every one of your emotions stirred up to a froth. A conscience, Dane decided, was one helluva nuisance.

"Okay," she said, her too-close-for-comfort voice drawing him back to reality. "Here's what you can do."

She handed him a mixing bowl and a large wooden spoon. "First, we mix the liquids."

Into the bowl, she broke an egg. With a wire whisk, she beat the egg while he held the bowl steady. Dane's heart jumped into the narrow passage of his throat. He'd never thought of cooking as an intimate activity. But, with Jessi less than a foot away, he was quickly learning to appreciate cooking in a way that was totally new and exciting.

"To the egg, we add one-half cup milk, two tablespoons oil, and one-half cup applesauce. Now, stir."

Although he didn't remember much of what he was doing,

he must have done it right because, moments later, she told him, "That's good. Now, we'll mix the dry ingredients. Just set that bowl over there on the counter."

She handed him a second bowl which he grasped tightly. While he wondered how it was possible to discern her unique wildflower fragrance among the cooking spices she used, Jessi mixed the dry ingredients.

"One and a quarter cup flour, one-half teaspoon baking powder, one-half teaspoon salt, one tablespoon sugar," she said.

He realized suddenly, that even the most mundane grocery list sounded exciting coming from Jessi's pale pink lips.

She left him holding the bowl while she checked the heat of her griddle. Obviously satisfied with what she found, she retrieved the egg and milk mixture and poured it into the bowl he held. "Okay, sheriff, you're on."

"What?" he mumbled inanely.

She smiled broadly, and nodded toward the bowl. "Stir."

Somewhere along the way, he noted with relief, she'd taken the bowl from his hands and spooned batter onto the grill. Like a wooden soldier, he stood at her side. *So close.* He lifted his hand, intent on touching the smooth slope of her throat. The urge to kiss the tiny freckles on her cheeks had him gritting his teeth and drawing what he hoped was a silent breath.

"Hand me that jar of honey," she told him.

Honey. The endearment went straight to his heart.

"What?"

"The honey. Over there on the counter".

Handing her the requested item, he admonished himself for not keeping his mind on the business at hand.

"Over low heat, we bring a quarter cup of honey to a slow boil. When bubbles form, we add one teaspoon orange juice and simmer a bit longer. It usually takes about five minutes."

"Five minutes," he repeated. *God, he'd never last another five minutes.*

Somehow he survived, despite his worries to the contrary. Jessi set an inviting table, complete with fresh flowers. Dane ate enough pancakes for two men. Jessi, he noticed, only picked at her breakfast.

Was she feeling the same things he was? he wondered. He truly hoped so. The thought of an ongoing relationship with Jessi Trainor made him—not surprisingly—hungry.

He'd just refused his third helping of pancakes when the telephone rang. "It's for you," Jessi told him, handing him the receiver.

Dane listened intently, shaking his head from time to time in silent emphasis. Moments later, he told her, "I have to go. Pike needs my signature on some forms."

"That's okay. I understand."

Dane raised his hand slowly. Stroking her cheek with the tip of one finger, he held it up for her inspection.

"What?" she asked.

"Honey," he told her.

Their gazes met. Warmly. Intimately. Slowly, he laid the tiny droplet of liquid gold on the tip of his tongue, then turned and walked away.

Four

"My, my, Jessi, you've certainly outdone yourself this time. Look at all this food."

Erline Patterson's high-pitched squeal of appreciation was music to Jessi's ears, quickly reminding her of how much she'd missed her landlady over the past couple of weeks.

"It's just a few test recipes," Jessi countered.

Truth be told, the two dozen muffins, three dozen low-fat brownies, and bowl of fruited chicken salad had nothing to do with her cookbook, and everything to do with the way she'd felt when Dane had left. The more exposure she had to Dane Logan, the more fortunate the residents of Oak Manor and Dane's deputies would be.

"On our way into town this morning we stopped for a few groceries. Mabel tells me you and Sheriff Logan delivered Mary's baby right out in the middle of nowhere. That so?"

"Yes, although my part in the delivery was minimal. If it hadn't been for Dane—"

"Dane? My, my, but you and our handsome sheriff have gotten right chummy since I've been gone."

"We're friends," Jessi said.

"Tsk, tsk, tsk," Erline admonished, "why if I were thirty

years younger, and didn't already have Abel, I'd be more than a *friend* to someone as downright sexy as Dane Logan. Why I remember Dane when he was coming up. We always said he was gonna be a heartbreaker.''

Jessi couldn't stiffle the giggle bubbling up from within and, when it finally surfaced, the infectious sound drew Erline's hoarse laughter as well.

''I couldn't agree with you more, Erline. I don't ever remember meeting anyone quite like Dane. Unfortunately, I've made a less than sterling impression on him. I'll be lucky if he doesn't steer a wide path around me from now on.''

''I'm sure whatever's happened between you and Dane won't deter him in the least. He's a very patient man. He's always been that way, even as a boy. Why he waited forever for—''

The sudden cessation of Erline's rambling caused Jessi to lift her head and meet the older woman's gaze.

''For . . .'' Jessi prompted.

Erline shrugged her shoulders, her frown rearranging her full and rosy cheeks. Reluctantly, she explained, ''Dane was engaged once. Marilyn was a big city girl at heart. Her family moved here when she was fifteen. She and Dane dated through high school, then for another four years at Michigan State. During their junior year . . . or was it senior year . . . anyway, Dane gave her a ring.'' Rubbing her fingertips across her forehead, Erline seemed to be searching her memory for other facts. ''The summer they graduated the entire town gave them a shower. It was the biggest event of the year. By October she'd run off to New York with a job offer from one of those fancy magazines. Dane tried to make a long distance romance work, but by the time he got to New York, she was involved with someone else. She even sold the engagement ring Dane gave her to put a downpayment on an apartment.''

Shaking her head for sympathetic emphasis, Erline added, ''The poor boy was devastated. Then, he was angry. So angry, in fact, he gave up his new job in Lansing and joined the army. Went off to some God-forsaken hell hole in the Middle East, he did. He came home four years later a changed man. He was quieter, more introspective. He quit working at impressing people. I guess he figured if we didn't like him for what he was, to heck with us. Of course, we'd always loved him just fine. The following year he took over for the retiring sheriff. That was five years ago and he's been with us ever since."

"How about since he's been home? Is there anyone special?"

"No, not that I know of anyway. Like I said, he's a quiet man and keeps to himself."

Jessi's shoulders lifted and fell on a deep sigh. "It really doesn't matter. The cookbook's almost done. I probably won't be staying much longer."

"I thought you promised to help out with the summer sports program over at the elementary school."

"Oh, right. I'd almost forgotten."

"I'm sure if you have to go, they'll forgive you."

"No, that won't be necessary. I promised I'd stay until school starts in late August. It's the least I can do for the kindness you've all shown me."

"Listen, sweetie, why don't you plan on coming down to supper tonight around six. I'll make my famous beef stew with dumplings."

"Sounds great." Surveying the results of her morning's efforts, Jessi added, "I'll bring desert."

"That'd be wonderful. Abel just loves your desserts. He says you can't even tell when they've got no sugar in them."

Dane snatched the fax from the machine as the last millimeter of paper slipped from the machine. According to the information contained in the state police communication, two escaped convicts were spotted in Harrisburg and heading west toward Traverse City. Brant Mills was dead center in their path.

"Armed robbery. Assault with a deadly weapon." Dane's words drew both Pike and Stevens toward the desk.

"What's up?" Pike asked.

Pushing the message across the desk, Dane explained, "According to this report, we have two escaped convicts headed this way. It might be best if we get out and go door to door warning folks."

"Why not the television?" Stevens asked.

"There's not enough time to get it out, and guarantee that everyone's watching."

Both Pike and Stevens nodded their agreement.

"I'll take the downtown area," Stevens suggested.

Dane knew that his deputy's concern lie in the fact that his family ran the bank less than two blocks away. If past experiences were anything to go by, the first place the escapees were likely to hit would be a money source.

"I'll take the east side of town," Pike offered.

Dane nodded, adding, "I'll take the west. Go out as far as the county line," Dane ordered, "we'll call those farther out if we have to. The state police have already notified the major television and radio stations in this area."

While Stevens set out on foot to cover the downtown core, Dane and Pike slid behind the wheel of their respective vehicles and set out to spread the words of warning often necessary in a rural community such as Brant Mills and surrounding Brant County. Pulling onto the first side street, Dane parked his car and began his door-to-door campaign.

By the time he'd reached his last stop, Dane had talked with half of the two hundred or so residents of Brant Mills, reiterating over and over again the necessity of locking doors, keeping the television set on, and calling the office at the first sign of something—or someone—out of the ordinary.

"Good morning, Dane," Erline Patterson greeted through the mesh of her screen door. A smile creased her features and lit her eyes. Pushing open the door, she invited, "Come on in." Her smile broadened when she asked, "What brings you around here today?"

Dane stepped into the foyer and began his speech at the same moment. "We're warning the entire town about two escaped convicts. They were last seen heading toward Traverse City, but they could have turned off in this direction."

"Are they armed?" she asked.

"The state police weren't sure. They didn't get guns off of the guards, but who knows how many accomplices they had meeting them on the outside. I'm sure you'll be safe if you follow a few simple suggestions.''

Nodding from time to time, Erline concentrated intently on his instructions.

"Is Jessi upstairs?" he asked.

"She should be—unless of course she needed something from the grocery store. She's—" Erline stopped short, then asked, "Would you like to come to dinner tonight, Dane. I know Abel's got those brochures you asked about. You know, the one's from the lodge. You thinking of taking a vacation?"

"Something like that," Dane answered absently, his thoughts upstairs minutes ahead of his body.

"How about dinner?"

He needed to get going, get out on the road. Yet, he couldn't be rude, so he said quickly, "Sure. What time?"

"Sixish, if that's okay."

He nodded, his mind wandering one flight up. "Six is fine. I'll see you then."

Erline locked the door behind him, then stood there watching him through the screen as he rounded the porch and headed toward the outside staircase. Dane wondered if Erline knew about how close he and Jessi had become.

Not so close, his conscience reminded. *You turn tail and run whenever things heat up. Face it Logan, you're a chicken. You can't face the thought of making another comittment. Another mistake.*

Once burned, twice—chicken fricassee.

Taking the stairs two at a time, his ascent to the landing took mere seconds—just long enough to admit his fears. The first rap of his knuckles against the wooden door frame went unanswered. His second knock, much louder than the first, netted the same result.

Jessi wasn't home.

An unexplainable chill ran down Dane's back. Finding Jessi, and making sure she was safe, suddenly became Dane's first priority.

* * *

"Good morning, Jessi," Mabel Stewart greeted from behind the counter of the general store.

"Morning, Mabel. How's your arthritis doing today?"

"Fine so far." Mabel shifted her bulky frame away from the wall and leaned forward. On a hushed whisper she asked, "Didn't you hear about the escaped convicts? You really shouldn't be out alone."

"I hadn't heard. I've been in the library researching some of the local herbs."

"Whenever you're ready, Jessi, I'll have my oldest son drive you back home."

Any intention Jessi might have had of voicing her refusal was quickly swallowed up by the look of concern on Mabel's face. Although she doubted she would need the assistance of an escort, Jessi said agreeably, "Sure, Mabel, I'll only be—"

The door opened suddenly, creaking on its hinges and banging against the window display. Just as quickly, it closed. The two men scanned the width and length of the store in a matter a seconds before the shorter of the two turned and bolted the door shut behind them.

Jessi slipped behind the counter and stood beside Mabel. Taking Mabel's hand, she squeezed tightly, offering whatever encouragement her grip could offer.

"Okay, ladies," the taller and uglier of the two men stated, "I'll take all the cash you got in the register and any you might have in your purses, too."

The gun he brandished in his hand spoke far louder than the man himself. In response, Mabel opened the cash register and stuffed the money in a brown paper bag.

"Now," the other man ordered, "your purses."

"I don't have one," Jessi told him. "Just a couple bucks in my pocket. You're welcome to them, though."

"My money, too," Mabel added, reaching into her apron pocket and withdrawing three one-dollar bills. "Please just take what you came for and go."

"Be obliged too, Ma'am. Soon as you fix us up some sand-wiches and fill two of them thermoses with coffee."

Jessi slipped behind the deli counter an set out to make the requested sandwiches. Mabel, in turn, took down two brand new thermoses and filled them with hot coffee from the ever-present pot, her hands shaking so badly she nearly dropped the full carafe.

Jessi's heart lodged in her throat with fear, for herself and for the older Mabel who was obviously on the verge of tears.

Oh, Dane, where are you? Jessi said to herself. *Where's the calvary now?*

To Jessi, the younger man said, "Hurry up over there, kid. I'm falling asleep waiting on you."

Jessi slapped a generous amount of mustard on all four pieces of bread then added turkey and ham and a slice of cheese. She was about to put the sandwiches together when a idea began forming in her head. She thought of her tote bag, and the packages it contained.

Lifting her head, she met the gaze of the first man. Smiling as sweetly as she could, she asked, "Could you hand me my tote bag?"

"Why?"

"I need my asthma medication. When I get upset, I have trouble breathing. I feel an attack coming on."

"Sure thing, lady. I don't want no sick broad on my hands. Here," the man said, extending the nylon mesh tote bag, "take it."

Jessi took the package of pills from the bag, holding them up so the man could see what she was taking. Unwrapping the over-the-counter drug, she popped one of the pills into her mouth and bent over the nearby water fountain for a drink to wash it down. With her back turned, she slipped the second bottle of pills from the sack. Her plan fully formed in her mind, she returned to the deli counter.

"You about done over there, toots?"

Jessi wasn't sure which man had spoke, but she nodded her head and assured them both, "Yes. I'm just cutting and wrap-ping the sandwiches."

All in all, the men spent less than ten minutes in the store, giving Jessi less than ten minutes to wonder if they meant what they said about getting what they came for and leaving peacefully. Still, the ten minutes seemed more like ten hours.

"Okay," Mabel reminded them, "you've got what you came for, please leave."

"Sure enough, lady. If you'd both be so kind as to stretch out on the floor behind the counter, we'll be outta here in two seconds flat. Don't get up until you've counted to one hundred. *Slowly.*"

Jessi and Mabel took their places on the floor, their hands entwined in support of one another. The door to the store opened and closed and the men were gone. When Jessi would have stood up, Mabel held her firmly in place with the weight of her arm.

"No, Jessi, let them get good and gone."

The door opened again. Both Jessi and Mabel drew a deep breath and held it. The next voice that spoke was the most welcome one Jessi had heard in ages.

"Mabel," Dane called, "are you here?"

"Oh, Dane," Mabel said on a rush, pushing herself to her feet in a surprisingly agile move. "Thank goodness you're here. We've been robbed."

The moment Jessi stood, she felt the heat of Dane's gaze on her cheeks. "Dane," she acknowledged.

"Jessi." *Thank God, you're safe.* "Are you both okay?"

"We're fine," Mabel replied for them both. "The thieves left two minutes ago, maybe less."

"Did you notice what they were driving?"

"No," Jessi explained, "they made us lie down on the floor before they left. We didn't see a thing."

"That's okay," Dane assured them. "Any description you can give us will help."

"I can do better than that."

Dane's gaze shifted to Jessi, a knot of apprehension settling firmly in his gut.

"How so, Jess?" he asked.

"I slipped them a mickey—I think that's the phrase."

Every internal warning device Dane had ever developed, every instinct he had ever honed, came vividly alive at the thought of what Jessi's words implied.

"What do you mean—a mickey?"

"I drugged them."

Dane drew a hand through his hair in an effort to calm the seventy-million nerve endings that seemed to be jumping around inside him. Inhaling deeply, he asked, "How did you drug them, Jessi?"

Mabel interrupted, "With your asthma medication. Was that how you done it?"

"I don't have asthma," Jessi explained. "Those cold pills were for Erline."

"Then how?" asked Dane.

"I also picked up a prescription for Mrs. McCurdy. Her sleeping pills. While I was making the sandwiches, I broke open four of the capsules and spread them evenly over the two sandwiches. The tiny grains melted right into the mustard."

Dane shook his head, his organized mind racing a mile a minute to assimilate everything Jessi said. In less time than it took to formulate a plan, he was out the door and on the car radio. Within minutes, every patrol car from Brant Mills, Milton, and the state police were combing the back roads for any sign of the convicts, either driving erratically or sleeping it off beside the road.

"Come on, Jessi" he said from the doorway of the store, "let's go."

"Go? I was going to stay and help Mabel straighten up."

"No you're not. Mabel's locking up until I can come back and take a report and get fingerprints. I'm driving you home."

"Yes, sir," she said sternly, spoiling her serious response with a quick smile.

Dane handed Jessi into the car, his arm on her elbow the warmest, most supportive thing she'd ever felt.

"You know, Jessi," he began after buckling himself in, "what you did was brave, but not necessarily smart. What if those jerks had caught you doctoring their food?"

The vision Dane's words made her shiver, coaxing her into admitting, "I hadn't thought of that. I—"

"It's okay, Jessi. No harm was done. As a matter of fact, assuming we catch these guys, you'll likely be touted as a heroine."

"I didn't do it for that, Dane. I only wanted—" Words stalled in her throat, stuck on a swift rush of emotion.

They drove to Jessi's apartment in silence. It wasn't until Dane parked the car in the driveway, unbuckled his seatbelt, and turned to face her, that he spoke.

"Listen, Jessi," he began. "I didn't mean to sound like I was yelling at you. I think what you did took both quick thinking and guts. If it had been anyone else but you, I'd have been slapping them on the back and congratulating them for their methods."

A look of genuine disappointment shadowed her beautiful face, causing him all sorts of unwanted emotions. He lifted her chin with the tip of one finger, capturing her gaze with his own.

"Then," he added firmly, "they'd get a lecture on the risks of doing something so fool-hearty."

After only a moment's hesitation, she asked, "What do I get?"

His own hesitation was even shorter than Jessi's. Shaking his head in self-denial of what he was about to admit, he leaned closer and told her, "What you've had since the first day I met you. My heart. And, this . . ."

Five

Jessi felt as if she were floating on air, transported somewhere between heaven and earth, gliding effortlessly on the cushion of Dane's kiss. Though not demanding, the insistent weight and pressure of his mouth held her in place. The light caress of his fingertips against her cheek stoked each of her five senses to life. When he broke the kiss and lifted his head, Jessi experienced the keenest sense of loss.

"I've got to go," he murmured, although he made no move to release the light hold he'd taken on her chin.

"I understand," she told him, although she didn't want to. What she wanted was to be held and kissed by Dane.

"I have to join the search."

Hesitantly, she agreed, "Yes, you do."

Leaning forward, he brushed his mouth across one cheek and then the other, coming to rest scant millimeters above her lips. His warm breath sent excitement skittering through her, inciting each and every nerve ending in her body to riot. When he kissed her, the slowly dying fires flared to life once more.

The kiss was a mixing and meshing of senses and tastes. When Jessi responded to Dane's gentle urging and opened her mouth for him, he filled her with his unique flavor. Clutching his shoulders for support, she did her best to return his ardor. No sooner had she touched his lips with her tongue when the kiss ended abruptly, Dane tearing his mouth from hers and pushing himself upright behind the steering wheel.

"Is something wrong? Didn't I do it right?"

He ran his fingers through his hair, then turned his hot gaze on her face. "No and yes. That's the problem—you did it too right."

How could anything be too right? she wondered.

With a quick flick of the key, he cranked the car's engine. This time, he really had to leave.

"I'll call you later," he told her.

She nodded, then slipped out the car door.

Jessi took the stairs two at a time, Dane's taste still fresh on her tongue. She'd promised to make dessert for tonight's dinner with the Pattersons. Rather dreamily, she wondered if she'd be able to concoct a dessert half as sweet as Dane's kiss.

Dane had barely reached highway ten when the call he'd been expecting came across the radio.

"This is unit one, over," he answered.

"This is Pike. The suspects have been spotted six miles east of the Milton turnoff on highway ten headed back toward town. A motorist with a car phone called in a drunk driver. The description he gave fit the car Chris saw pulling out of town right after the robbery at Mabel's."

While Pike gave his report, Dane engaged his siren, and flicked on his lights, a plan of action already forming in his mind. "I'm on my way," he confirmed, "and headed straight for them. What's your position?"

"We're about five miles behind them and closing in."

"Well boys," Dane joked, hoping a bit of humor would lighten the serious situation they faced. "Looks like I'll meet you in the middle."

Less than two minutes later, he saw the car in question coming toward him. The vehicle swayed precariously from side to side on the two lane highway, swerving from one gravel shoulder to the other and back again. In addition to having to face off with the two suspects, Dane quickly assessed the possibilities of becoming a motoring statistic. The best he could hope for, he realized, was that the suspect's car would land in a ditch before he got to them.

Dane's wish was not to be granted, as moment's later the two cars were less than five hundred feet from each other and both traveling at a high rate of speed. Dane eased off the gas, doing his best to anticipate the driver's next maneuver. Surprisingly, just short of the mid-point between the two cars, the other car stopped. Close to the soft shoulder of the road, the front wheels of the vehicle sank into the loose gravel.

Dane pulled his patrol car across the road, effectively blocking any hope of escape in that direction. If his calculations were correct, his deputies would be bringing up the rear in less than a minute.

Slowly, Dane approached the non-descript brown car, his service revolver drawn and ready. No interior movement was visable from where he stood, so he settled in beside the right front fender, keeping the hood of the car between himself and the suspects.

"Okay, fellows," he called loudly, "step out of the car with your hands on your head.

The short expletive shouted by one of the men was slurred, yet easily identifiable.

"If you want to make this difficult, we'll wait for my deputies. Once you've got us coming at you from all sides, you might have wished you'd come out peacefully."

"Okay, okay," one of the men mumbled. Opening the passenger door, he literally fell out of the car and lay sprawled on the ground.

"What the hell's going on?" he mumbled, "I can't hold my head up."

"You idiot," the other man yelled, "we've been drugged. The stupid little girl did this when she was makin' those sandwiches. Sheriff," he yelled, "you tell the broad she's gonna regret what she did."

Dane's anger flared, but he controlled it quickly. It wouldn't do to let his temper rule his thoughts. That was the way mistakes were made.

Pike and Stevens pulled up behind the suspect's car, angling their patrol car across the road just as Dane had.

"The state patrol is about three minutes away," Pike called.

Another vivid expletive escaped the driver's side of the car.

"Well, fellow," Dane appealed, "are you willing to give it up now?"

Dane could see the motion of the man's head as he nodded it. A moment later, the door opened and the man stepped out, his hands linked in place on top of his head. Cautiously, Dane approached the man, his attention going momentarily to the second man. Thankfully, he was out cold.

"Okay, that's good," Dane coached, "now face the car. Place your hands on the roof, and spread your legs."

The man followed Dane's orders to the letter. Dane holstered his gun and stepped forward. He was reaching for his cuffs when the man spun around and swung his clasped hands in Dane's direction. On instinct, Dane blocked the blow, shoving the man backward toward the car. On what Dane suspected to be one last rush of adrenalin, the man pressed forward, falling into Dane and knocking them both to the ground.

Pike rushed to Dane's side and was in the process of reaching for the suspect's shirt collar to pull him up when Dane reversed their positions, putting himself on the top. Taking a fistful of the suspect's shirt, he drew him upward until they were face-to-face. The urge to pummel the man with his bare fists was overwhelming, especially for the threat he'd issued toward Jessi just minutes before. Yet, Dane resisted the temptation his anger offered.

The man struggled only a moment longer before collapsing back onto the ground. As he drifted into unconsciousness, he spit out one final, partial, threat, "Tell the little . . ." In the next instant, he was still, as unthreatening as his partner.

"I'll be damned," Pike muttered, "she did it. She actually did it."

"I don't want anything about Jessi's part in this to be leaked to either the press, or the public."

"But—"

"You heard me," he said. "This guy threatened Jessi. I don't want to worry about him having some friends who might want revenge."

Pike nodded his understanding.

"Good," Dane acknowledged. "Now, let's wrap this up, and get these pond scum turned over to the state police."

"In a hurry?" Pike asked.

Glancing at his watch, Dane shook his head. "I'll never make my dinner invitation now, anyway."

"Jessi?" his deputy guessed.

"No, Abel and Erline."

"Too bad."

Yeah, Dane agreed silently. *Too bad.*

Dane stepped beneath the shower, moving back and forth beneath the hot, pounding, spray, doing his best to ease the kinks from his overworked muscles. He'd thought of calling Erline, and extending his apologies, but first he needed to wash away the accumulated sweat and dirt resulting from his scuffle with the second convict.

Between the actual capture, the mountain of paperwork, and the release to the state police, Dane hadn't had the opportunity to call and beg off the impromptu invitation.

He dipped his head beneath the shower's spray, and closed his eyes to keep out the shampoo, his thoughts going quickly—automatically—to Jessi, and the memory of those few stolen kisses; those precious few moments of paradise. He could have gone on kissing her for minutes . . . hours . . . but for the obligations he couldn't shirk.

Liar! Duty could have waited for one more kiss. You panicked, that's all.

Dane shook his head in silent denial.

She's not Marilyn, his conscience reminded him. *Jessi's sweet. Innocent. Jessi'd never leave you for some jerk in New York.*

Maybe not, but she's not here forever, she said so herself.

She's only here long enough to write her cookbook. Long enough to spark my interest.

Long enough for you to fall in love?

That, Dane conceded to his badgering conscience, hadn't taken long at all.

"I'm really sorry, Dane," Erline said in response to his issued apology, "we were looking forward to seeing you tonight. And, I don't mind sayin', you missed one heck of a meal."

"I—" Dane began only to be stopped short by Erline's next words.

"And, Jessi made the most delicious dessert. Carmel Apple Surprise, I think she called it."

"Jessi was there?" he heard himself ask.

"She still is. As a matter of fact, we were just thinking of having a second dessert and a cup of coffee. You wouldn't care to join us, would you?"

"Well . . ." *Go on,* his conscience urged, *you know you want to go.* "Sure," he said, "I'll be there in ten minutes."

The bright lights of the Patterson house shone like a welcoming beacon all the way down the street. In deference to the beautiful summer night, Dane had elected to walk, covering the three-quarter mile distance in mere minutes. He'd no sooner set foot on the veranda, when Erline opened the screen door and ushered him inside.

"I'm so glad you made it, Dane. We don't see near enough of you. Abel was just saying so earlier today."

Dane followed his hostess into the parlor. Abel was settled comfortably in his easychair, his glasses perched on his nose, his evening newspaper laying in his lap, and his attention given to the woman at his side.

Jessi.

Curled up on the end of the two-seater sofa, she and Abel were pouring over the brochures she held in her hands. Brochures of far-off exciting places.

"Someday, I'd like to go here," Dane heard her say, the words making his heart skip a beat.

Where are you going, Jessi? How much longer do we have?

She looked up from the mounds of brightly colored papers,

her gaze clashing with his, her brilliant green eyes widening and lighting with the same fire he'd seen when they'd kissed.

"Hi," he mumbled inanely, wishing he had issued a more impressive greeting.

"Hi," she said in return, her smile making the single word a warm benediction.

"Abel," Dane acknowledged with a nod. "How was vacation?"

"Just great, Dane. The fishing was excellent."

"I hope you brought home a few for us less fortunate souls who can't seem to find time for a vacation."

An hour and two cups of coffee later, Dane walked Jessi to her door, his arm enclosing her shoulders in a firm, guiding, hold. A cool evening breeze rustled the tendrils of hair at her ears, blowing them across her cheeks. The first stroke of Dane's fingertips pushed aside the flyaway hair and sent a shiver clear down to her toes.

"Your Carmel Suprise was delicious, Jessi."

"Thank—"

The tentative brush of his lips against hers muffled her reply. When he added, "but not nearly as delicious as you," Jessi melted—much like the warm carmel sauce in her recipe—from the inside out.

"Dane?"

"Hmm . . ."

"What did you mean by our first kisses being *too good?* How can anything that feels so right, not be perfect?"

Lacing his fingers together behind her back, he drew her forward into his embrace. In response, she lifted her arms, linking her hands behind his neck; capturing as she'd been captured.

"I'm not sure what it is, Jessi, that makes you so special. All I know is that I want to hold you, kiss you, make . . ."

"Make love to me?" she asked hopefully.

His sigh spoke eloquently of his frustration. "To a point . . . yes . . . I want to make love to you."

"But not all the way," she guessed.

"Jessi," he whispered, nodding toward the stairway and the yard beneath them, "this is not the time, or place to discuss—"

"You could come inside," she suggested tentatively.

"No, I can't."

"You can't?"

"Won't," he stated firmly.

"Why not?"

"Because I don't trust myself where you're concerned."

"*I* trust you."

The warmth in her eyes underlined her words, telling him in no uncertain terms that she would willingly make love with him. Willingly give him what he suspected no man had ever had before.

"Don't, Jessi. Don't trust me."

His words obviously made her nervous. "But why?" she asked.

"Because, Jessi, I want you."

"And I want you," she countered.

"I'm sorry, Jessi," he told her, "but I'm not ready for a permanent attachment." *No matter how much I care.*

Squaring her shoulders in proud defiance, she told him, "I didn't say anything about permanent."

He couldn't help but admire her spunk, nor could he resist the urge to brush the brave words from her lips with the end of his thumb. Just before he lowered his head to take the kiss she so willingly offered, he told her, "I'm still old fashioned, Jessi. I believe some things should be saved for the wedding night."

"Some things?"

"Your innocence, for one. My sanity, for another."

"But—"

Pressing his fingertips to her lips, he sealed in whatever protest she'd been about to make. When he lifted his hand, he slid his slightly parted lips into place, tasting her, devouring her in his mind; cherishing her with his heart.

Someday, I'll take more than this, Jessi. Someday I'll have it all.

Jessi arrived at the local community center at half-past eight the next morning. Karen was there, along with two teachers from the elementary school who had offered to help with the summer program. Three high school student volunteers were expected later.

"Morning, Jess," Karen greeted. "We've got coffee and donuts."

"Coffee sounds good," Jessi acknowledged, "but I think I'll pass on the donuts."

"Suit yourself," the teacher Jessi knew as Sally Parker told her. "We're just now starting to make a list of the activities we want to offer."

Ralph Sparks, the other teacher, added, "So far we've got swimming. I'll do that, along with one of the older students. Karen's down for arts and crafts. She'll need a student for that."

"What about my home ec class?" Sally asked. "I'll surely need help there."

"We only have enough budget for three students. You and Jessi'll have to share the third one," Ralph suggested. "What are you planning for your activity, Jessi?"

Jessi spared a quick, anxious, look at Karen. Spurred on by her friend's nod of approval, she told them, "Gymnastics. I thought I'd coach gymnastics."

"I take it you've got some experience," Sally guessed.

"A little," Jessi admitted.

Immediately, Karen added, "A little? Why, Jessi's—"

Quickly, Jessi interrupted, "I've got enough for a beginner's class. All we need is some basic equipment. Abel's agreed to build me some low balance beams."

"I think there's a pommel horse we can borrow from the high school," Ralph added helpfully.

"That would be great, and surely enough for what I intend to teach."

The remainder of the morning was spent in developing schedules, setting aside time to train their assistants, and a general sharing of information. Jessi promised Sally that she'd find some very basic cookie recipes among her files, and Karen promised to ask a few of the more agile residents of Oak Manor if they'd mind coming by the center and serving as extra hands.

"That is, of course," Ralph pointed out, "if we get the response we're expecting."

"I've already got twenty-six names on my list," Sally reminded them. "By the end of the week, we'll probably have fifty."

"How will they be transported to the park for swimming?" Jessi asked.

"Dane and a few of the others will drive them back and forth."

"The community spirit in this town is overwhelming," Jessi told them honestly. "I hope wherever I go from here will be half as nice."

By Thursday, as predicted, they had nearly fifty eager participants in Brant Mills first-ever summer activities program. It was decided among the planning committee that they would divide the children among the four areas, and then rotate each week so that all the children were able to take part in all the activities.

Late that day, after the others had gone, Jessi set out her newly built equipment, slipped out of her sneakers, and stepped up onto the wooden beam.

It's been so long. So very, very long. What if you fall?

Don't be ridiculous, she silently admonished her taunting inner voice, it's only six inches to the ground.

Not to be discouraged, the voice asked, *What if you fail the children? How will you feel if you let them down?*

Defiantly, she took her first step, then a second, daring her conscience to force her off the beam. Long forgotten memories sifted slowly through her mind. The crowds, the tight-knit group of competitors, the long, long hours of practice. Her third, fourth, and fifth step came naturally. On the sixth step, she faltered, but regained her footing within a blink of an eye. Turning on her toes, she returned to her original starting spot and stepped off the beam. Although her heart was pounding a fierce tatoo within her chest, she'd done it. She'd beat the beam, and temporarily stiffled her tormenting conscience.

Ha! That wasn't a beam. That wasn't even high enough to be a railroad tie. Why don't you try a real beam? Why don't—

"Jessi?"

The sound of Dane's voice sank into her heart, warming her where her teasing inner voice had left her cold.

"Hello, Dane."

"Hi, Jess. Abel sent the rest of the beams. They're out in the truck. He sent you a surprise, as well."

"A surprise?"

Dane's deputies came through the door at that moment, each carrying one end of a balance beam mounted on two permanent sawhorse legs. Her attention drawn to the well-made piece of equipment, Jessi absently waved as the deputies deposited the equipment and left.

Look, Jessi. A beam—not a railroad tie.

Unaware of the panic that had risen within her, Dane explained, "Abel thought that—in case you have some promising students—you might want to upgrade them to something a little more daring."

"I'll be sure and thank him," she said, swallowing past the lump in her throat and talking past the dryness in her mouth.

"Is something wrong?" Dane asked.

She hesitated, amazed by his ability to read her so easily. "No," she finally insisted, "of course not. I just wouldn't want any of the children to get hurt, that's all."

You just don't want anyone to ask for a sample of your expertise. What will you do then, Jessi?

Her thoughts were once again interrupted by Dane's low, husky voice, "Jessi?"

"Yes?"

"How about taking in a movie Saturday night."

"A movie?"

"Yeah," he teased, "you know—big screen, dark room. Popcorn, with tons of butter." Wagging his eyebrows expressively, he added, "Stolen kisses in the dark."

"Sounds great—especially the stolen kisses part. How about I fix us some dinner first?"

"I'd never turn down an opportunity to sample your cooking," he assured her. "Especially one of your luscious desserts."

"Good, I know just the dessert to tempt your taste buds."

Grinning, he asked innocently, "What would that be?"

Crooking her finger, she drew him forward for a sample of the sweetest kiss he had ever tasted.

Six

Jessi tied back her hair with a pink ribbon. No sooner had the last strand of hair fallen into place when she was yanking out the ribbon and replacing it with another. Nothing looked right. Not her hair, her dress, or even the stupid ribbon she'd selected to help tame her fly-away curls.

With impatient hands, she smoothed down the skirt of her sundress, settling the soft pleats in place over her hips and thighs. Selecting another ribbon, the same shade of blue as the stripes in her dress, she lifted her hair off her neck and secured the satin strip in place. Despite the firm bow she tied, whisps of hair escaped at her nape and cheeks.

"This is ridiculous," she muttered to her mirrored reflection. "What's so special about this date that you can't seem to do anything right?"

You know what's special, her conscience taunted. *Dane Logan. He's special.* Silently, Jessi admitted that—for once—she and her inner-voice were in complete accord.

At half-past six, Dane's familiar knock sounded against the door to her apartment. Making one last check in the mirror on her way by, Jessi answered the door.

"Hello, Dane," she greeted.

"Hello," he returned, his gaze flaring, his slow perusal leaving a trail of warmth over her hair, her face, her bare shoulders.

"Come in, please," she invited, holding the door open and stepping back to allow him admittance.

Dane came forward, following her lead, holding her mesmerized with his smile. Just as Jessi moved to close the door, Dane reached out as well, their hands meeting at the brass knob, her's first, his second, joined in a casual mating that sent tingles coursing through Jessi's arm.

Disengaging her hand from beneath his, Jessi led the way to the small sitting room just off the kitchen. A white rattan loveseat took up most of one wall. On the opposite wall was a table and shelves which held Jessi's computer and reference books. In one corner was an over-stuffed chair, its brocade cushion faded with age.

"Have a seat," Jessi told him, motioning toward the end of the loveseat. "I'll get us something to drink."

Cautiously, it seemed, Dane settled onto the loveseat. The woven wood creaked loudly beneath him.

"What would you like?" she called from the kitchen. "I have wine coolers, wine, or soda pop."

"Wine will be fine."

"Red or white?"

"Red."

While Jessi poured their drinks, Dane took a moment to study the small parlor, his attention drawn time and again to the expensive computer in the corner of the room. *High tech.* Very high tech.

"Nice computer set up," he commented loud enough for her to hear.

"Thank you," she said from just over his shoulder.

In her hands she held a tray with their drinks, red wine for him, a can of diet cola for herself. Also on the tray was a plate of cheese, crackers, and fruit wedges. Jessi set the tray down on the coffee table and then seated herself at the opposite end of the loveseat.

Dane inhaled the bouquet of the wine, letting its aroma waft slowly through his senses, much the same as his gaze was taking in the length of Jessi's bare legs and sandaled feet. When he licked his lips in anticipation of both the wine and the woman, she unconsciously mimicked his movements. The innocent gesture had him gulping down his first mouthful of wine.

"So," he said, his voice made hoarse by the hastily swallowed wine, "what's for supper?"

"Ceasar salad, chicken kiev, white asparagus in mustard sauce, and mushroomed potatoes."

"Sounds great," he told her.

"If you're hungry we can eat now."

Oh, I'm hungry all right. But this nagging ache in the pit of my stomach has nothing to do with food. "In a few minutes. I'd hoped we could talk awhile first."

"Talk?" Jessi asked. "I always thought men avoided talking whenever possible."

"Guys on the make avoid heavy conversation," he admitted, then added sincerely, "I'm not on the make, Jessi. I enjoy talking to you." Her eyes lit with uncertainty, and he told her, "I like talking to you very much."

"Is there something special you want to talk about?"

"Yes. I want to talk about you."

"Me? There's nothing special about me."

Dane reached out and captured a flyaway strand of her hair, placing it behind her ear. His gaze held her mesmerized, the nod of his head slow and deliberate. "Yes there is, Jessi. To me you're special."

She shook her head, vigorously denying his claim. She didn't want to be special. Being special meant having to do everything right. Having people expect something from you. *Of you.* She'd been special once. And once had been one time too many.

"I'm nobody special, Dane, just a cookbook author who enjoys traveling around the country and writing books."

"What about your family? Don't you miss them while your traveling?"

Shrugging her shoulders, she explained, "I miss Steve—my brother. And, I'm dying to see his new baby. I miss my mom, too. Although we don't always get along."

''No one sees eye to eye with their parents all the time. I know I don't.''

''Where do your parents live?'' she asked, genuinely interested, she realized, in anything Dane had to say.

''They run an Inn just outside Traverse City. I get up to see them once a month. They close the Inn for the month of December and come back to Brant Mills.''

''Do they stay with you?''

''Yes. Technically, it's still their house. I just live there.''

''Miss Chalmers pointed your house out to me during one of our walks. It's lovely, especially the yard.''

''I pay a couple of school kids to mow the lawn and trim the hedges. The flowers are my neighbor's contribution. Penny loves working in the garden.''

''Penny Beeler?'' Jessi asked.

''Yes. Do you know Penny?''

Jessi nodded, her thoughts shifting to the tall, attractive, blonde. ''I've met her. Miss Chalmers introduced us.''

''Penny's a widow,'' Dane pointed out. ''Her husband was killed in a boating accident last summer.''

''That's a shame,'' Jessi commiserated, ''she's so young.''

''Yes,'' he agreed, ''she is.''

Jessi didn't want to think about the lovely widowed Penny being Dane's next door neighbor, yet she couldn't help but picture the two of them together. Penny's tall frame would compliment Dane's height much better than Jessi's own five-foot nothing. The golden blonde of Penny's hair nearly matched Dane's perfectly. They'd have beautiful . . .

''Jessi?''

Dane's softly whispered call drew her from her thoughts. ''Yes?'' she whispered back.

''I'm not interested in Penny, if that's what you're thinking.''

Jessi's embarrassment fueled the warmth of her cheeks and the urge to bite into her lip to keep from acknowledging how accurately he had read her mind.

''Oh,'' was all she could manage before her train of thought was completely derailed by the touch of Dane's fingertips against her chin, the glide of his thumb across her lower lip.

"As a matter of fact, the only woman I'm interested in is you."

"Really?"

Dane lifted her chin with his fingertips, aligning their gazes one to the other. "Really," he told her. Lowering his head, he sealed his claim with a kiss.

With Dane's lips so thoroughly caressing hers, Jessi had little time to think about anything but the heady flavor of his kiss. Just like the other kisses they'd shared, this one sent wave after wave of excitement through her, each tremor a kaleidescope of sensation. Slowly, Dane lifted his head, his retreat drawing Jessi's moan. The tangy aroma of his aftershave filled her head, along with an insistent buzz that she couldn't seem to shake.

"I think," Dane mumbled against her lips, "that your oven timer is going off."

Drawing a deep breath to calm her jangled nerves, Jessi excused herself and made a hasty retreat to the kitchen. Dane, she noticed, followed closely in her footsteps, bringing with him every scent . . . every emotion . . . she'd tried to leave behind in the parlor. The very notion that his kisses could leave her so senseless was mind boggling. No man had ever made her feel this way. No other person in her life had ever made her feel so wanted. So loved.

"Supper's ready," she told him, her voice only the slightest bit unsteady.

"Good. I'm starving."

They ate in silence, except for the compliments Dane gave with each new taste. Jessi accepted his words of praise with timidly issued "thanks", all the while wondering if he was as nervous as she; as aware of the intimacy of sharing a candlelight dinner.

Once the meal was over, and the dishes cleared, Dane suggested they leave for Milton. "The movie starts in a little over an hour. We wouldn't want to be late."

"No," she agreed, "we wouldn't. Just let me get my purse."

Dane seated Jessi in his truck and closed the door between them. He wasn't exactly sure what was wrong with him but, ever since that one innocent kiss in Jessi's parlor, he couldn't seem to catch his breath. Each and every movement Jessi made drew his attention. Her perfume, though subtle, filled his head with visions of spring flowers.

Climbing behind the wheel, he fastened his seatbelt and started the engine. The low growl of the motor filled the cab of the truck, humming along in perfect rhythm, setting the pace for their drive.

Other than to point out areas of interest along the way, Dane couldn't think of a single topic worthy of conversation. As a matter of fact, he realized suddenly, the last thing he wanted to do with Jessi was talk. Other, more interesting, activities came quickly to mind, followed by all the reasons he couldn't partake in those same activities.

She's too innocent. You'll likely frighten her away with the strength of your desire.

I'd never hurt her, he argued back.

Not intentionally, maybe. But . . .

"Dane?"

"Hmm," he mumbled, his thoughts caught up in his internal argument.

"I'm not sure, but didn't we just pass the exit for Milton?"

Dane glanced quickly in Jessi's direction and then back at the highway. How could he have missed an exit he took on a regular basis?

You know very well how, his conscience reminded him. *Try getting your mind off kissing Jessi and back on the road.*

Dane pulled off the highway and onto the next small side road, slowing the truck to a halt. He checked the traffic, and found that he could easily pull back onto the highway as he'd planned. Yet, for some unexplainable reason, he didn't turn. Instead, he shoved the gearshift into park and reached for Jessi, unbuckling her seatbelt and drawing her forward in one fluid motion. Willingly, it seemed, she melted into his outstretched arms.

Go ahead, his conscience prompted. *Kiss her. Maybe if you do, you'll be able to get your mind back on the road where it belongs.*

"Jessi," he whispered, "dear God but I need to kiss you."

Jessi didn't answer with words, but with the softness of her lips pressed to his. She tasted of cherries jubilee and diet soda. Impatient for a second, deeper, taste, he nibbled non-too-gently on her lower lip, encouraging her to open to him. She did so, as willingly as she'd come into his arms. As he slipped his tongue into her welcoming mouth, he felt a moment of panic. A realization that—from this point on—nothing would ever be the same.

Dane threaded his fingers through Jessi's hair, tugging the silky strands free of their confining ribbon, massaging her scalp in rhythm with his probing tongue. When he should have eased her away, he drew her closer, until she lay across his lap, cradled tightly in his arms. Only then, with her softly rounded breasts pressed against his chest, did he remember where they were. Who they were.

Along with this one moment of conscience came the realization that—at that moment—he was exactly who, and where, he wanted to be. A man, held securely in the embrace of the woman he loves.

Reaching behind Jessi's back, he fumbled for the ignition key and killed the engine. "Jeezus, Jessi, but you taste good," he mumbled, more to himself than to her. Before she could answer, he took another taste of her mouth. And then another.

Jessi's initial reaction was one of appreciation. Appreciation for Dane's gentleness. His finesse. His unique taste. Those first reactions were quickly replaced by a strong and undeniable hunger. A passion to be held and loved by Dane Logan. Stretched out across his lap, she could feel every taut muscle, every ridge and ripple. Every hard plane. His . . .

"Dane," she softly said, "we're going to be late for the movie."

"Mmm, I know." With those few, lazily drawled words, he slid his hand to just beneath her breast, his fingertips straining toward the tightly-drawn crest.

"Oh," she gasped, tiny frissons of electricity sizzling through her veins, followed by an overwhelming flood of warmth.

Dane buried his face in the wild mass of hair Jessi could never seem to tame, his huskily whispered words inciting riot within her highly sensitized body. The sound of his raggedly drawn breath echoed her own gasps for air.

Tentatively, it seemed, Dane brushed his fingers across the swell of her breast, testing both her resistance and her complacency with his measured caress. She had no intention of stopping his gentle explorations. When he lifted his hand slightly, she cupped his fingers in her own hand and pressed them back to her breast.

Lost in their sensual explorations, time slipped by. Jessi suddenly realized the sky around them had darkened with every passing minute, the bright illumination of the moon and stars gilded their joined hands and highlighted the emotions so plainly etched on Dane's handsome face.

As plain as day, his expression said, *he wanted her.*

That thought made Jessi giddy. Bold. Pressing her mouth to his, she licked her lips and his, the warm, thoroughly sensual, motion parting Dane's lips so that she could take control of the kiss.

When she finished her tentative explorations, Dane lifted his head and gasped, "Jessi. Oh, baby, don't do that."

Empowered by his words, Jessi flicked her tongue out. Tasting him. Teasing him. "What?" she asked, feining innocence. "Am I doing something wrong?"

He shook his head, and growled deep in his throat. "No, Jessi, you're doing everything right." Laying his head back against the rear window of the narrow cab, he lifted her higher, drew her closer.

"Do it again, Jessi, just like before."

Eagerly, Jessi repeated the kiss.

"Now," he whispered against her lips, "deeper."

Jessi followed his request, dipping into his mouth, extracting his enticing flavor with the tip of her tongue. When she would have broken the kiss, Dane held her close, giving back to her what she had just taken.

Caught up in the hottest, most sexual kiss, she had ever experienced, Jessi met him taste for taste. They dueled, one the aggressor, the other the willing submissive. They parried, changing roles at the skip of a heartbeat. Only when they could no longer deny their need for air, did they end the kiss.

Dane raised his head, his eyes glazed over with desire that even Jessi, with her limited experience, could recognize. The moon shone in his eyes, its brilliant glow interrupted by an on-again-off-again flash of light.

Dane muttered something unintelligible beneath his breath and, in the next moment, righted Jessi in the seat. She opened her mouth to ask what was wrong—what mistake she'd made—when she noticed the direction of Dane's gaze, and the hurried way he was smoothing back his finger-tossled hair. From the rear a car approached, its bright red and white lights signaling its arrival.

"Great," Dane mumbled. "Just what we need."

"What is it?" Jessi asked.

"Some of Brant County's finest are about to admonish us for parking along side the road like a couple of randy teenagers."

Jessi did her best to smother a giggle.

"What's so funny?" he asked.

"Wasn't that just exactly what we were doing?"

Before he could answer, a tap came to the side window of the truck. Obligingly, Dane rolled down the window. Another deputy, Jessi noticed, stood at her window as well.

"Evening, Dane," Deputy Stevens greeted. "You having car trouble?"

"No," Dane answered, his voice a study in control.

"You and Miss Trainor staking out the area for possible crooks?" asked the other deputy.

"Very funny, Martin," Dane said sarcastically. "If you must know, we were talking."

"Well then, don't let us interfere with your . . . talkin'. We'll just get back in the car, make our turn, and head back to town."

"You do that," Dane suggested.

Both deputies doffed their hats in Jessi's direction, then Stevens added, "Night Dane. Night Miss Trainor. See you in the office tomorrow, Sheriff."

Jessi couldn't help the round of laughter that escaped her

throat with the deputies retreat. Dane's only reaction was a very serious scowl, a menacing look that would have frightened someone who didn't know him well.

"You know, Dane," she said, doing her best to cajole him into a better mood, "you shouldn't take things so seriously."

"Really?" he grumbled. "Just how should I take being caught necking on a dark side road by my own deputies."

"Well, for starters," she informed him, "you could lose that scowl?"

Crossing his arms over his chest, he glared at her. Stubbornly, he asked, "And, if I don't?"

"I might be forced to kiss it away."

He gave her another menacing look before his frown gave way to a teasing smile. "And I might just let you," he retaliated. "Except . . ."

"Except what?"

"Except, then, we'd be back in another clinch."

Jessi smiled, inwardly trembling at the thought. "Would that be so bad?" she asked.

Dane reached out and ran his thumb over her kiss-swollen lips, then admitted, "No, Jessi, that wouldn't be bad at all. As a matter of fact, it would be wonderful." Lowering his hand back to his side, he added, "Unfortunately, the night patrols in Brant County run like clockwork. If we stay here much longer, the next set of flashing lights will belong to the state police."

Seven

"You got caught doing what?" Karen's high pitched cry was a mixture of both astonishment and amusement, filling the room and echoing off the walls. "I can't believe it," she added for emphasis, her words drawing Jessi's ire.

Jessi poured Karen a cup of coffee, then asked, "What is it you can't believe? That Dane and I would be parked somewhere? Or, that we got caught?"

Shrugging, Karen said, "Both. I guess. Somehow I hadn't pictured you as Dane's type. And, I'd never have thought of our strictly-by-the-book sheriff as the type to go parking on a dark road in his own county. And get caught! He must have been mortified."

Him? What about me? Jessi wanted to ask. *What about my feelings? You're supposed to be my friend.*

"He took it quite well," Jessi confided. "Other than a bit of good-natured teasing, neither deputy said much. Never once did either of them mention the fact that we were parked on a dirt road in the middle of nowhere, or, that we shouldn't be there."

"I wonder how much ribbing he took the next day in the office?" Karen asked.

"I don't know," Jessi admitted. "I haven't talked to him since he dropped me off on Saturday night."

"Four whole days and not a word?"

Not a word, Jessi repeated silently to herself. "No. I suppose he's been busy."

"Yeah," Karen agreed, "I suppose you're right."

Jessi could hear the doubt in Karen's voice, as well as read it in her expression. Lifting her cup, Karen took a sip of the freshly brewed coffee.

"How's registration going for the summer activity program?" Jessi asked, wanting . . . no needing . . . to divert the conversation to less sensitive ground.

"We'll have fifty-four kids when we begin next week."

"That's great, and much better than you'd expected."

Over coffee, they discussed the success of the program, Mary Taylor's baby, the beautiful weather—anything and everything but Dane.

Her coffee cup empty, Karen stood to leave, her smile once again old-friend genuine. "I'll see you Friday for our final meeting before the start of the program. I expect everyone'll be there, even Mayor Byrne."

"I'll be there."

Jessi shut the screen door behind her friend, slipping the latch lock into place. After checking to make sure that she'd turned the coffee pot off, and put the milk back in the fridge, she went into the sitting room and booted up her computer. Flipping through her floppy disks, she selected the one marked *Muffins.* Once the booting process was complete, she slipped the floppy into the disk drive and recalled the correct file.

Despite the uniqueness of the single recipe she'd subdivided into nearly two dozen variations, Jessi couldn't get her thoughts organized, or her heart set on perfecting yet another muffin clone. Her thoughts, like her heart, were filled with Dane, and with the realization that he hadn't bothered to call, or come by, since their date.

Had their being caught—with their guard down—embarrassed him to the point that he was angry with her? Had he gotten in trouble somewhere along the line? Both possibilities worried her.

Automatically, Jessi exchanged her recipe file for another. *Her therapy disk,* as she'd dubbed it. Slipping the floppy into place, she called up the directory and selected the file marked *Feelings.*

The hard drive whirred and clicked, finally spitting forth Jessi's therapy. Her heart's undertaking. A catharsis for what ailed her—up to a point. A mixture of a personal diary and her feeble attempts at poetry, *Feelings,* was about emotion. Deep, heart-tugging emotion.

Love.

The last entry, made the day after her date with Dane, was a definitive description of what it was like to be in love.

With Dane.

Dane finished his normal afternoon routines, giving each an every detail of his report a quick going over. He was due at the school at half past one, and the last thing he wanted was to be late.

She'll be there.

I know that.

How will you explain not having called?

I'll think of something.

Why not just admit you've got cold feet? Why not admit you can't face the fact that, once summer's over, she'll be leaving? Just like Marilyn.

Shut up!

The teasing voice inside Dane's head erupted in laughter, confident of its hold on Dane's thoughts and insecurities.

Karen, Jessi noticed, was greeting each member of the committee as they came through the door. The room was filling up fast, with only Dane among the missing. Even Mayor Byrne was already there, despite his usual penchant for tardiness. The young mayor was currently occupying the seat next to Jessi, and bending her ear with his latest mayorial accomplishment. Jessi glanced in Karen's direction, making a silent plea for rescue.

Karen was about to shut the door, when Dane slipped inside. "Sorry, folks," he apologized to the entire group at the same time, "I was held up by a last minute telephone call."

"It's okay," Karen assured him, "we haven't started yet. I think there's a seat left beside me."

Dane followed Karen to the far end of the table, taking his place and pouring himself a glass of water. Jessi watched him closely, hoping that he'd lift his head and meet her gaze. He didn't, and Jessi felt the slight as distinctly as if he'd deliberately turned his back on her.

Karen called the meeting to order, and asked each of the program participants to give their final report. Sally Parker reported on the total number of registrants, and outlined what her part of the program would entail. Ralph Sparks reviewed his program plan, as did Karen. Dane confirmed that two of the town's merchants had promised the use of their company vans for transporting the children to the lake for swimming lessons, and that he and Pike would do the driving.

"What about liability insurance?" Mayor Byrne asked.

Dane explained, "That's all being underwritten by Jake Hopkins. He's given us a short term policy for the duration of the program, and then written off the expense as a contribution."

Mayor Byrne's secretary, there to take official minutes, offered to send Mr. Hopkins a thank you note for his generous contribution.

"That would be nice," Karen commented. "Thank you." After consulting her agenda, Karen asked, "Jessi will you give your report now?"

Jessi lifted her head, her gaze immediately going to Dane. For the first time since the meeting started, their eyes met. All the words she'd so concisely woven together for her report ran together—sent into oblivion by Dane's blank expression. Where was his smile? Any reaction, she noted, would be better than a cold, unfeeling, stare.

"Jessi?" Karen prompted, drawing Jessi from thought to reality with one quick tug.

With an apologetic smile, Jessi began, "Abel Patterson has generously supplied us with mini-balance beams. Just six inches from the floor, they'll pose no threat to the children's safety, while still allowing them the feeling of practicing on actual equipment. We've borrowed a pommel horse from the high school, along with some tumbling mats and sixteen inch practice balls. Using these supplies, I'll be able to teach the children the basics of elementary gymnastics."

Mayor Byrne asked, "If you don't mind telling us, Jessi dear, what experience do you have with teaching gymnastics."

Dane seethed. *Jessi dear?* Where did Byrne get off calling his woman, Jessi dear? Dane was suddenly overcome with the urge to set the mayor straight. Only the realization that he'd undoubtably make a fool of himself, and embarrass Jessi, kept him in his seat.

His woman, the silent claim echoed through his head as, tentatively, Jessi relayed her qualifications.

"I've had fourteen years of gymnastics training myself, beginning when I was four and up until shortly after my eighteenth birthday."

Murmurs went from one person to the next, each member of the committee as curious as the other. Jessi's gaze, Dane noticed, went nervously to Karen's. Slowly, Karen nodded, offering Jessi her unspoken support. Again, Dane felt a pang of jealousy, an uncertain response demanding that he be Jessi's support; the person to offer her encouragement.

Right, Fricassee. You gotta get the feathers out of your mouth first. Dane shook his head, dislodging his conscience and zeroing in on Jessi's softly spoken words.

"I was being groomed for the Olympics," she admitted, her words interrupted by a round of whispered ooo's and ah's. "From grade school on up, I was fortunate enough to train with some of the world's finest coaches. The training I received from them would more than qualify me to teach entry-level gymnastics."

Ralph Sparks asked the question Dane imagined was poised

on everyone's lips. "What made you quit, Jessi? Why would you give all that up to write cookbooks?"

Jessi laughed, but the sound was lifeless, much the same as the translucence of her pale skin and the dull glaze of her usually brilliant green eyes. Dane's heart ached, yet he wasn't sure why.

"I didn't give it up, Ralph," she stated simply. "It gave me up. Or, more precisely, my body gave up on me. A month before the last set of Nationals, I injured my knee. It didn't seem like a serious injury at the time. Yet, after three weeks of rest, and scores of specialists, I still couldn't put weight on my leg. The Nationals came and went and, along with them, my chances at the Olympics."

"What about the following Olympics?" Sally Parker asked.

Like the others gathered around the table, Sally's concern was written clearly on her face. Jessi, Dane realized, had made many friends since coming to Brant Mills, and those friends were eager to commiserate with her over her past.

"By then I was over the hill, so to speak. Even at eighteen, I was pushing it. Besides, my knee never really recovered to full strength. Even now, six years later, I'm still plagued with an occasional twinge."

The meeting continued on for about forty minutes, finishing with Byrne's usual glad handing and credit-taking speech. The reverend said a prayer of thanksgiving for the generosity of those who had volunteered, and for the safekeeping of the children. Karen adjourned the meeting at three-thirty.

Slowly, but surely, the room emptied, leaving only Karen and Jessi and Dane.

Karen glanced from Dane to Jessi and back to Dane. Gathering her briefcase in her hand, she stood. "Well, I guess I'd better be going, too. If I'm not back at the Manor by four, Harry Rollins will be leading a mutiny on the kitchen."

"Can I go with you and help out?" Jessi asked.

"Everything's under control," Karen told her, "but thanks for offering."

Karen closed the door behind her, leaving Dane and Jessi alone. Jessi, Dane noticed, fidgeted with the pile of papers in front of her, her head bent over the notes she had taken through-out the meeting.

She's nervous.

Dane drew a deep breath and let it out on a sigh. *We need to talk, Jessi.*

Don't think it. Say it.

"Jessi?"

When she lifted her head, he saw the first stirrings of a smile, the simple reflex drawing his own grin in return.

"Jeez, Jessi," he said with relief, "are you as embarrassed about what happened as I am?"

"Not really embarrassed," she admitted, "just concerned."

"Concerned?"

"I was afraid you'd gotten in trouble. I mean ... I thought ..."

Jessi's explanation stalled, suspended in limbo by the light weight of Dane's fingertips against her chin. He lifted her head up until their gazes met. He was shaking his head, his smile broad and infinitely sexy.

"No trouble, Jessi, just a helluva lot of teasing from Pike and the boys."

"Then why didn't you call?"

"I was kind of waiting for things to die down. I didn't want to run the risk of my deputies seeing us together and ..."

"And?" she prompted.

"Actually, I was scared."

"Scared? Somehow, I can't picture you being afraid of any-thing."

"Not afraid, Jessi. Scared. There's a heck of a lot of differ-ence."

"There is?" she asked.

Dane gathered one of her hands in his and slowly massaged her fingers. The gentle motion of his hands should have been soothing, yet Jessi's breath caught with each glide of his fingers over hers. When he drew the same hand to his lips for a fleeting kiss, Jessi felt as if she were free falling from the world's highest balance beam, unsure of whether or not she had a mat beneath her, or if her feet would ever hit the ground.

"Afraid is a reaction to an outside stimuli. Something you can see. Touch. Like an escaped criminal, or a flasher," he told her. "Scared is an internal reaction, more emotional than physical."

"What do you have to be scared of with me?"

"I'm scared of how you make me feel. I haven't felt anything as powerful as this in ages. If ever. And, I'm not quite sure what to do about it."

Tell him, Jessi. Better yet, show him.

Jessi stood, her head barely reaching Dane's chin. Placing her hands on his shoulders for balance, she lifted herself onto her tiptoes. "You could start, I suppose, with a kiss."

Gladly, it seemed, he acquiesced to her suggestion.

Dane drove Jessi home, letting her off in the driveway.

"Cup of coffee?" she offered.

"No, sorry. Shift change is at five. I need to get back to the office."

"Some other time, then."

"Some time *soon*. I want to see you again."

Jessi let herself into the apartment, her senses still alive with the memory of Dane's kiss. Her thoughts lost on Dane, she didn't realize she had company until she nearly tripped over the briefcase sitting in the middle of the kitchen floor.

"It's about time you got home," he said.

Startled, Jessi put a hand to her chest, pressing against her wildly beating heart. "You scared the daylights out of me." His deep laugh drew her forward and she threw herself in his outstretched arms. "How'd you get in here anyway?" she asked.

"Your landlady. After I'd introduced myself, gone through the third degree, and shown my identification, she finally relented and let me in."

"How long can you stay? Where's Liz, and the baby?"

"Just until tomorrow. I'm scheduled to attend a weekend conference in Traverse City. Liz and Caitlan are at home."

"Just one day? Are you sure?"

"Yes, sweetheart, I'm sure." Lifting her frown with his thumb, he asked, "Now, where around here can a guy take his favorite girl out for supper?"

Dane gave his report to the oncoming shift, anxious to get home. He'd change into his running shorts, he reasoned, then he'd go for a jog. The possibility of seeing Jessi occurred to him, and his pulse raced in anticipation.

God, but he'd hated ending what they'd begun in the deserted school room. She'd tasted so good. So fresh. *So willing.* That thought alone should have scared him off. Yet, it hadn't been the possibility that Jessi would welcome further advances that had halted the tentative exploration of his kiss. It had been the call of duty; the realization that his men were expecting him back at the office to give report and complete the shift change.

How commendable, Sheriff.

Back off, Dane ordered. *I've got control of the situation. You'll not intimidate me any more—not where Jessi's concerned.*

Dane stepped off the wooden porch in front of his office. The dying sun blinded him for a moment, and he lifted his hand to shade his eyes. That was when he saw her.

Jessi. And a man. A tall, handsome stranger.

They were walking hand-in-hand down the mainstreet of town, stopping at each and every storefront, laughing like old friends. Lovers. Dane was about to cross the road and ask for an introduction, when the dark-haired stranger slipped his arm around Jessi's shoulders and squeezed.

In response, she hugged him back. The genuinely heartfelt gesture sent Dane's jealous reflex into overdrive. And, knowing himself as well as he did, his anger into oblivion. If he approached Jessi and her friend now, the words of introduction he'd utter wouldn't be fit to be heard by any living human being.

Before she could see him, Dane slipped between his office and the drug store. Out of sight. And, *obviously,* already out of mind. He set his course for home, walking off the worst of his anger, slowly cooling off. Calming down.

He was through the gate and onto the porch before he realized he'd left his truck behind.

Jessi wondered where Dane had gotten to. His truck was parked in front of the office, yet Pike said he'd left nearly half an hour earlier.

"So, where's this wonderful sheriff of yours?"

She shrugged, and explained, "I'm not sure. The deputy said he'd gone home for the day. Yet, his truck's right here."

"Maybe he had other business in town."

"I suppose," she conceded. "I really wanted to introduce you. I think you'll like Dane. I know he'll like you."

"You're sure?" he prompted teasingly.

"Of course. I've already told him—you're the world's greatest brother."

Eight

Jessi put away the Monopoly board and cleared the dishes from the kitchen table while Steve took a blanket and two pillows from the linen closet and carried them into the sitting room.

"Are you sure you won't take the bed?" Jessi asked. "I'll fit a whole lot better on that hide-a-bed chair than you will."

"No thanks, Sis. I'll be fine." In an effort to convince himself, it seemed, he tested the twin-sized mattress by pressing down on it with his hand.

"If you're sure—"

Laying back against the pillows, he told her, "I'm sure, Jessi. Now, go to bed."

Jessi leaned over her sprawled-out brother and kissed his cheek. "Good night, Steve."

"Good night, Jess."

On her way to her room, Jessi paused and confessed, "I'm glad you came for a visit. Even if it was only for a few hours."

"I'm glad I came, too. I've missed you."

"And I'm sorry you missed meeting Dane."

"Me too, Jess. He sounds like a great guy."

* * *

Dane ran like a man possessed. One mile, two miles, his heart pounding in rhythm with his churning thoughts. The more he tried to displace Jessi from his thoughts, the deeper she delved. The harder he ran, the more vivid his memories. The farther he ran, the closer he came to the woman he was trying to ignore.

He'd done his best to avoid the beautifully flowered and treed street, the long, winding road leading to Able Patterson's house. Yet, no matter which way he ran, his feet turned back toward Elmwood Avenue.

The lights in Jessi's apartment went off, one by one, ending with her bedroom. Dane leaned against the thick trunk of a nearby tree, breathing heavily from both the exertion of his run, and a new and infinitely debilitating emotion. *Jealousy.*

The man's jeep sat in the driveway, proof that—even though the lights were out—he was still there. Dane strained to identify the strange vehicle, wondering who this man was and where he'd come from. Edging closer to the driveway, Dane quickly memorized the combination of numbers and letters on the jeep's license plate.

He waited a while longer, hoping that the man would leave. When he didn't, Dane turned and jogged back home, more lonely, more hurt, than he could ever remember being. Not even his ill-fated relationship with Marilyn could have prepared him for the anger and pain he felt at the possibility of Jessi sharing her bed with another man.

What are you so worried about anyway? Isn't this the excuse you've been looking for?

Dammit, leave me alone.

First, it was, "she's too young". Then, "too innocent." Now, you're not so sure, are you? Maybe, she's just like Marilyn after all.

No, not Jessi.

Fine. That puts us right back where we started. You're just plain scared. Scared of commitment. Scared of being jilted. Worst of all, scared of feeling.

* * *

By the time Jessi woke the next morning, Steve was already on his way to his weekend conference. He'd made coffee and toast for himself, and left Jessi a note, thanking her for putting him up for the night.

Jessi washed the cup and plate her brother had left behind, then poured herself a mug of coffee and spread homemade jam over a hunk of French bread. While she sipped and nibbled, her thoughts ran rampant through her head. Where had Dane been last night? Had he been called in on his weekend off?

Had he spent the evening in some kind of danger?

You're being a bit melodramatic, aren't you?

No, just concerned.

The need to see him, and assure herself of his well being, hastened her steps.

Jessi dressed in one of her prettiest summer dresses, then set out on her ususal Saturday morning shopping trip. The town market would be in full swing today, along with the weekend flea market. The combination farmer's and flea markets drew people all the way from Grayling which was forty miles to the east.

What it also drew, Jessi admitted to herself, was security. Namely, Dane and his deputies. The thought of seeing Dane did strange things to Jessi's emotions, setting loose a swarm of butterflys inside her stomach, turning her temperature up a full degree.

Well, Dane noted rather unreasonably, at least she's alone.

What did you expect? It was all you could do to stay in your office and not give her overnight guest a police escort out of town.

Yeah, Dane agreed in bitter silence, obviously the man had gotten what he wanted and moved on. The realization that he might possibly be wrong about Jessi angered him more than the thought of her with another man.

Liar!

Clenching his hands into fists, Dane argued back. I told you to leave me alone, dammit. It doesn't matter.

Like hell it doesn't. You can't take your eyes off her. Can you?

Rebelliously, Dane looked away, only to have his attention drawn back to Jessi and her long, flyaway, red curls., Damn, but she was beautiful!

"Hello, Dane."

Karen's voice startled Dane out of the tug of war he was playing with his conscience.

"Hi, Karen. How's it going?"

"How's what going?"

Shrugging, he said, "Anything, everything. Hell, I don't know."

"Something got your dander up, Sheriff?" Karen asked.

"Nothing you can do anything about."

His gaze wandered back to Jessi, his deep sigh revealing more than he would have liked.

"She's a great person, you know," Karen stated.

"Yeah, I know," he agreed. "It's a shame she's got a boyfriend."

"A boyfriend? Jessi?" Adamantly, Karen shook her head. "I've known Jessi since we were kids. I'd be the first to know if she had a boyfriend."

"I saw him with my own two eyes. And . . ."

"And?" Karen prompted.

"Never mind. It's not important."

"Well, Dane, I think you're wrong. As a matter of fact, I *know* you're wrong. There's only one man Jessi's interested in, and *that's you.*"

Dane wanted to refute Karen's claim. To tell her how he'd seen for himself the proof of Jessi's late night liaison. Yet, he couldn't. Wouldn't. To do so would be admitting that he'd spied on her—an admission of guilt, of jealousy. He wasn't ready to make either.

"If I were you, Sheriff," Karen continued, "I'd get over there and straighten things out. Before both of you lose something important.'' In a show of empathy, she patted Dane's arm then turned and strolled away

Without Karen as a buffer, he could feel Jessi's eyes on him, watching him as closely as he'd once been watching her. Even from a distance, he could see the play of conflicting emotions cross her delicate features. He could see her confusion, as clearly as he felt his own. She smiled, tentatively, it seemed. Then she lifted her hand and waved, the motion of her curled fingertips slight and nearly indiscernable. Curiously, he wondered what she was thinking.

There, see, he's fine. All your worrying was for nothing.

He certainly looks fine, doesn't he?

He's the most handsome man we've ever met.

I thought we'd agreed looks weren't important.

Jessi could hear the voice inside herself chuckling.

That's true, but they certainly don't hurt.

Jessi lifted her head, her gaze meeting Dane's across the crowded town square. He smiled. Mesmerized by his intense expression, she waited as he closed the distance between them.

''Morning, Jessi,'' he greeted.

''Good morning, Dane.''

''How are you?''

''I'm fine, and you?''

Small talk. God, but he hated small talk. ''Pike says you came by the office last night looking for me. Did you want something special?''

''I had someone I wanted you to meet.''

Before Jessi could elaborate, Dane admitted, ''I saw him.''

''You did? Why didn't you say hello?''

''I didn't want to interrupt anything.''

Something in the sharp tone of Dane's voice set off a warning signal in Jessi's head.

''Excuse me?''

''I said, I didn't want to interrupt anything. The two of you were pretty cozy strolling arm in arm, sharing the occasional hug, a private joke.''

''I can't believe you're—''

''Can't believe what?'' he interrupted. ''That I'm jealous?

That I can't stand the thought of knowing the two of you spent the night together?''

Jessi could feel the quick uprising of her temper in the warm and heavy flush of her cheeks. "We spent the night together," she repeated, her voice a study in patience she really didn't feel.

"Yeah," he bit out, not the least bit concerned that he was admitting to having spied on her. "The lights went out about eleven thirty."

"And, just where were you when my lights went out?"

"I was out for a run. I happened by the house and noticed a strange jeep in the driveway. It didn't take me long to match the jeep with the man I'd seen with his arms wrapped around you earlier."

"His arms weren't *wrapped* around me," she stated. "At least not in the way you mean."

"Just how do I mean it, Jessi?"

"As if it's something lewd. Dirty."

Dane raked his fingers through his hair, then reached out and grasped Jessi by the arm, drawing her back behind the shelter of a nearby elm tree.

"What do you expect me to think when the fellow spends the night in your apartment?"

Incredulous, Jessi shook her head, and said, "I don't believe this. I really don't. How dare you spy on me?"

"I was only doing my job," he defended. "This guy's a stranger in town. He—''

"He's none of your damned business," she whispered emphatically.

"Listen, Jessi—''

Punching her forefinger into his chest for emphasis, she told him, "No, you listen. I don't know what you think you saw, but you couldn't be more wrong. The *fellow* you saw me with last night—all night—was my brother. He was on his way to Traverse City for a weekend conference and stopped for the night. If you hadn't let your narrow-minded jealousy get in the way, you might have come up to the apartment and introduced yourself."

"But . . . I thought—"

"I know what you thought, Dane Logan. You thought I was sleeping around." Again she pushed against his chest with her finger. "Just because I willingly accepted a few of your kisses doesn't make me a tramp. I don't—"

This time Dane interrupted. "I know."

"You know what?" she asked skeptically.

"I know you don't sleep around. If I'd have been thinking straight last night, I would have realized that myself—maybe even in time to meet your brother. I should never have doubted your innocence."

Jessi felt her cheeks flush a warmer crimson, this time from embarrassment rather than anger. "My innocence is none of your business, either. And, another thing—"

"I'm sorry."

"What?"

"I said," he repeated, his expression contrite, and his smile devastating, "I'm sorry. I was acting like a jealous idiot."

"Were you?"

"Were I what? An idiot?"

"No. Jealous. Really jealous."

Lifting her chin with the tips of his fingers, he aligned their gazes. Nodding, he confirmed, "Extremely."

Jessi wet her lips with the fleeting touch of her tongue, her throat dry and her thoughts incoherent at best. Her skin tingled where Dane's fingers touched, and her heart ran an uneven race within her chest. He was going to kiss her. And, as angry as she should have been at his underhanded spying, she was going to let him.

Bending forward, Dane pressed his mouth to Jessi's, the soft, silky, feel of her full lips a sensual branding he wouldn't soon forget. The milling shoppers and loud noise surrounding them receded into the background, leaving behind only the sound of his and her mixed breaths, the feel of her lips, and the taste that was exclusively Jessi's.

From somewhere behind them, a discreet and familiar cough ended Dane's short trip to paradise, and slowly he lifted his head. "Yeah, Pike," he mumbled, "what is it?"

"Sorry, Dane, but you're needed in the office. There's a message coming across from Lansing's DMV."

"Just take it off the fax and put it in my top drawer. It's not important."

"It says, *RUSH*," Pike pointed out.

Dane stepped away from Jessi and turned to face his deputy. "It's not important any more. The problem's been solved."

Pike shrugged his broad shoulders and straightened his hat on his head, clearly confused yet not willing to question his boss's word.

"Okay," Pike agreed, "I'm not worried about it if you're not."

By the time Pike had made his way into the crowd, Dane had turned back to meet Jessi's inquirying gaze. "Okay," he admitted grudgingly, "I had his plates checked out. But that was before—"

"It's okay, Dane. Really." Her smile underscored her words. "As a matter of fact," she admitted, "it's kind of nice to think that you were jealous of my brother. After all, he is a handsome devil."

"Yeah, I suppose," Dane agreed grudgingly.

As if she could read the hidden recesses of his mind, she told him, "But not quite as handsome as you, Sheriff."

By three thirty that afternoon the vendors had packed up their wares and headed home. The town's small sanitation department worked diligently on the after-market clean up, and Jessi and Dane sat on a nearby bench enjoying the first few moments of peace and quiet since early that morning.

"So, Jessi," Dane asked, "I understand your cookbook's almost done."

"One more chapter, give or take a couple of recipes."

"Where to next?" he asked.

"I've been mulling over the idea of moving to New York. I could continue to write cookbooks, and maybe start that catering business I've always wanted. New York or not, though, it's time to settle down."

"How about Brant Mills? You've made some good friends here."

"I'd have to think about it some. I kind of pictured myself settling down in a big city."

"But why New York?"

"Because I've always lived in small towns. Big cities were always part of the competition venue, yet I never got to really *see* them. I want to experience something . . . exciting."

Dane frowned, and Jessi wondered what he was thinking. She didn't have long to second-guess before he said, "Take my word for it, Jess, there's nothing that great about New York, or any other big city for that matter. At least in a small town, you're a real person. In the city, you're no more than a stranger in a big pool of strangers."

Jessi opened her mouth to speak, but shut it without uttering a word. The expression on Dane's face was all she needed to see to convince her that he spoke from experience.

By the time Dane got to New York, she'd taken up with someone else. He was heartbroken . . .

Erline's words came back in a rush, a bitter pill to be swallowed. Jessi wanted to kick herself for being so thoughtless.

Somedays, Jessi, she admonished silently, *you just don't know when to shut up!*

Monday brought the official opening of the summer activities program. Arriving at the school half an hour early, Jessi was met by a contingent of willing workers and excited children. The enthusiasm everyone exhibited made Jessi glad that she'd set out a definite plan, mapping out her strategy for the gymnastics class over a pot of hot tea the night before. The exercise in planning had also helped keep her mind off Dane, and the conversation they'd had Saturday in the park. If his words were anything to go by, he really wanted her to stay in Brant Mills.

Or, he was just making conversation, her conscience supplied.

Don't forget, Jessi retaliated, he admitted he was jealous over Steve. In her mind's eye, Jessi could picture her erstwhile conscience giving a shrug of temporary defeat. The thought made her smile.

"Good morning, boys and girls," Karen's greeting broke through the children's excitement, quieting down even the loudest child. "Today we will be working together in the gymnasium as one large group. There are color coded cards for each of you to fill out. These will be your name badges and will be printed with information that will help us make sure that you are taking part in the right activity at the right time. Tomorrow, you will begin with your first scheduled activity."

A girl with pigtails and freckles raised her hand. When Karen indicated she could speak, the girl asked, "My mom wants to know what time I'll be home each day."

"Activities will end at three-thirty each day. Parents who have arranged transportation for their children should expect them by four."

Karen's explanations, along with the children's questions, went on for another twenty minutes. All during that time, Jessi leaned casually against the nearby wall, studying the group of children one by one. A young boy of no more than seven drew her attention on more than one occasion. There was something about him that tugged at Jessi's heartstrings. Jessi couldn't help but wonder who he was, and why she'd never seen him before today.

Engrossed in her study of the boy, she didn't notice when Dane came to stand beside her.

"Harley Masters," Dane whispered, nearly causing Jessi to jump out of her skin with surprise.

"What?" she gasped.

"The boy who's caught your eye. His name is Harley Masters."

Harley Masters. Although she didn't understand why, Jessi knew she and young Harley were destined to become friends.

Dane settled in behind his desk. Steepling his fingers together, he leaned against his joined hands and closed his eyes in thought. He'd spent a good part of the morning at the school helping put together name badges, and making sure each and every child understood which activity they would be participating in beginning Tuesday morning.

Jessi, he'd noticed, had spent most of her morning with Harley Masters. Dane understood her fascination with the big-eyed, sad-faced, little boy because he'd once felt the same pull toward the youngster himself. He didn't feel that way any longer. Harley had seen to that. When Dane had offered friendship, the boy had made it clear, in no uncertain terms, that he wanted to be left alone. Just like Alex. Where Harley and Alex Masters were concerned, the old saying, *Like Father, Like Son*, hit the mark.

Opening the log book on his desk, Dane filtered through the weekend reports. There were two minor accident reports, both taking place just outside the town line, and one incident of vandalism involving a couple of teenagers from nearby Milton. Nothing of major importance, yet commonplace for a small town.

On the bottom of the pile sat the report from the Department of Motor Vehicles on the plates he'd run at six-thirty Saturday morning. Staring out his office window that morning, he'd watched the mysterious jeep pull out of town. At the time, his unwarranted jealousy had taken precidence over everything else, and he called in a request for vehicle identification. Now, two days later, his feelings of guilt firmly in place, Dane crumpled the piece of paper into a ball and held it tightly in his fist.

Aren't you even going to look at it?

It's not necessary, he told his inner-voice. It was Jessi's brother all along.

Don't you wanna make sure?

In spite of the fact that he trusted Jessi, Dane found himself prying open the crumpled ball, and pressing out the creases with the flat of his hand. As he'd known it would, the DMV confirmed that the jeep in question belonged to Steven Trainor, Stuartdale, Minnesota.

Jessi's brother, just as she had claimed. The relief he felt was overwhelming.

Nine

Jessi helped the next participant onto the balance beam. "Now, Chrissy," Jessi instructed, "hold your arms out straight." Lifting the girl's arms upward, Jessi said, "Yes, just like that."

The six-year-old smiled broadly, her gap-toothed grin adding character to her freckled face.

Friday. The first week was nearly over. Jessi couldn't wait to get home and take a shower, brew herself a cup of tea, and curl up with a good book. She ached. The kids, so full of life and mischief, had worn her out. One by one, they'd learned the very basics of gymnastics.

All except for Harley. Harley had progressed quickly. From mat, to pommel horse, to paralell bars, he'd far surpassed the others. Possessed of near-perfect balance, he'd astounded everyone with his natural ability.

Standing at her side, Harley asked, "Can I help you put things away?"

"You've stayed every night this week," she reminded him. "It's time someone else helped."

"Nobody else wants to. Just me."

"Okay," she agreed, "you can help. Start with the mats."

Jessi stared after the boy as he tugged and pulled and pushed until he'd put everything in its proper place. She could feel her heart flutter, then soften. She was becoming far too attached to Harley, and he to her. When it was time to leave, their parting would be painful—nearly as painful as leaving Dane.

Within a half-hour of quiting time, Harley and Jessi had cleaned up the entire practice area, putting everything but the heavy pommel horse in the storage closets inside the gymnasium.

"You'd better go home now, Harley," Jessi told him. "Thanks for your help."

"Yes, Ma'am. I'll see you next week."

"Next week you're scheduled for swimming."

"I don't want to swim," he said rather defiantly. "I want to learn more about gymnastics."

"We'll see, but I'm not making promises. It'll depend on getting parental approval."

The boy grinned, and Jessi realized it was the first smile she'd seen on Harley's thin face. "Bye, Miss Trainor."

Waving her hand, she called out, "Goodbye, Harley. Have a nice weekend."

"You've made quite a friend there."

Low and seductive, Dane's voice wrapped around Jessi like a warm blanket on a cold morning, enclosing her. Holding her. Tempting her to stay when she should get moving.

"Hello, Dane. How'd today's swimming lessons go?"

"Fine." Lifting one end of the pommel horse, he dragged it across the floor and toward the storage closet. "A couple of the kids had to be reprimanded for swimming out past the markers but, otherwise, things went smoothly."

Pulling the equipment behind him, he stepped into the closet. Jessi followed. On the wall was a wire basket full of basketballs, its lid ajar. Dane reached up and closed the heavy cover.

"Where's the wooden peg we use to keep this closed?" he asked.

Jessi glanced around the room. Leaning over, she picked up the narrow sliver of wood.

"Here," she said, producing the requested peg.

Too late, she realized, the wood was being used as a doorstop. Before she could react, the door closed, and the lock clicked into place, sealing them in semi-darkness, the room's only illumination coming from a very small skylight above their heads.

If he'd thought Jessi wouldn't get angry, Dane would have laughed at the ridiculousness of their situation. Here they were, half past five in the evening, not a soul in sight, and trapped in tight quarters.

He did the only logical thing. He kissed her.

She put up a token protest at first, pressing her hands against his chest, pushing gently. Her resistence lasted only as long as it took to part her lips with his tongue. The moment he gained entry into her mouth, she quit pushing. Instead, she raked her nails across his shirt, scoring the fabric in rhythmic motions that slowly unraveled his composure. Within moments, he was aroused.

"You did this on purpose, didn't you?" he asked.

"No," she protested, "of course not. I didn't—"

He swallowed her words with his mouth, stilling her excuses with tongue. When she trembled, he reciprocated with a shiver that rocked him clear down to the soles of his feet.

"We've got to get out of here," he stated firmly. "Otherwise, I won't be responsible for whatever happens."

Running her hand across the front of his shirt and over his broad shoulders, she touched his cheek lightly before sifting her fingertips through his short hair. Drawing his mouth down to hers, she demanded, "Shut up, Sheriff, and kiss me."

Gladly, he followed her command. Aligning their bodies one to the other, he drew her closer until the only thing between them was their thin cotton shirts, her shorts and his denim jeans. And heat. Alluring, seductive, enticing heat.

Dane withstood as much as his body could take before he grasped Jessi's arms and set her away. Breathing heavily, he told her, "Let me take a look at this door while I've still got some light to work with."

The lock was standard issue, he realized with some relief, and matched that of the front door and the principal's office.

And, like the other locks, it could only be opened from the outside.

Third key to the left of your truck key, right?

Yes, he admitted.

To get outside, all he had to do was climb up to the skylight, prop it open from the inside, and climb out. Once outside, he could get back in and open the storage room door. In less than ten minutes, he and Jessi could be out of the cramped storeroom and on their way home.

Separate homes.

The thought kept him from making that first move. He couldn't do it. Not yet. Not until he'd had his fill of Jessi's kisses. Not until he'd pushed himself, and his sanity, to the edge.

Turning back to face her, he said, "Come here, sweetheart."

She balked at first, and he wondered if he'd hurt her feelings by pushing her away moments before. "Jessi—"

Jessi cupped her hand over Dane's mouth, catching his intended apology in her palm. "Can you get us out of here?"

He nodded.

"When?" she asked.

"Whenever we want."

Stepping forward, she wrapped her arms around his waist, and snuggled into his arms. "How about sometime tomorrow morning?"

Chuckling, he corrected, "How about right after a few more kisses?"

Her sigh washed over him, warming his lips, filling his senses.

"All right, if you insist," she agreed, "but I like my idea better."

The incessant ringing of the telephone woke Jessi out of a sound sleep. Immediately, her heart started pounding. Who would be calling her at six on a Sunday morning? Reaching for the telephone, Jessi brushed the hair out of her eyes and wiggled her way into a sitting position on the side of her bed.

"Hello?"

"Good morning, beautiful."

"Good morning, Dane."

"I thought I might be able to interest you in an all-day outing. I was thinking of driving up past Traverse City and doing some hiking. Are you interested?"

"Yes, very. Give me twenty minutes to get ready."

"Okay, see you then." She was about to hang up when he added, "Jessi?"

"Yes?"

"Wear jeans and sturdy shoes. Bring a lightweight jacket. I'll take care of everything else."

"Okay. See you—"

He interuptted, "Jessi?"

Something in the hurried rush of his words made her anxious, and she answered, "What is it, Dane?"

"I . . . ah . . ." He cleared his throat, the sound echoing through the telephone wires. "I'll be there in twenty minutes. Be ready. I can't wait to get on the road."

Dane forced himself to slow down. He was acting like a school boy on his first date, for heaven's sake. Barely ten minutes had passed since he'd hung up the telephone, yet he was already dressed and out the door. He purposely stood beside his truck and surveyed the surrounding street, anything to slow him down. Less than a heartbeat later, he was jumping into the truck and cranking the engine, his patience worn as thin as new ice on a deep lake.

"You're going about this all wrong," he scolded out loud. "If you can't control yourself any better than this, you'll both be in trouble. Hell, you sounded like a blabbering idiot on the telephone. It was a small wonder you could manage to string two sentences together."

For once, his conscience climbed the opposite side of the internal fence. *Take it easy, Sheriff. Once a man's discovered how far he's fallen, it's difficult to articulate even the simpliest of sentences. You're being far too hard on yourself.*

"Where the hell did you come from?"

I've always been in here. You just couldn't find me for all your doubts. Remember one important point.

"Yeah?" Dane mumbled.

Jessi's not anything like Marilyn. Be careful. You can hurt Jessi as deeply as you were once hurt.

Pulling into the Patterson's driveway, Dane offered one last word to his conscience. "Thanks."

You're welcome.

"Where did you say we were going?" Jessi asked.

"Rockland. There are some real nice hiking trails in the state park."

Jessi relaxed back into the seat, her gaze affixed to the passing scenery, the lush trees and expansive fields of every imaginable crop a testimony to Michigan's rich and fertile land. To the right was an apple orchard. To the left, at least ten acres of pear trees. The pungent aroma of pregnant fruit trees filtered in through the partially-opened window.

"It's so beautiful," she commented to no one in particular.

"I've always thought so," Dane agreed. "Like you, I'd thought of moving somewhere else numerous times, of experiencing the bright lights and the big city. I'd gone so far as to travel to New York."

"To catch up with Marilyn?" The words were out before Jessi could stop them. Too late, she realized he would know she'd listened to the local gossip.

"Yes," was all he said. "It wasn't one of my brighter moves." Running his free hand slowly across the dashboard, he asked, "How much did Erline tell you?"

"Most likely all she knew," Jessi admitted. "She says you were high school sweethearts."

"High school, college. I thought we'd be together forever. I was a Grade-A, number-one, fool."

"I'm sure no one else thought that."

"It hurt like hell at the time."

"Does it still hurt?"

He shook his head, and told her, "No. Whatever was once there is as gone as it can get."

"Good."

"What about you, Jessi? Is there a man lurking somewhere in your past?"

"I've dated off and on, but there's never been anyone serious. There's never . . ."

Jessi let the admission trail off unfinished, leaving Dane to draw his own conclusions.

"I told you once that I'd bet my badge on your innocence."

"I remember. It embarrassed me at the time, but it doesn't anymore."

"It doesn't?"

"No." Before he could ask her, she volunteered, "Unconsciously, I suppose, I've saved myself for the right man."

"A husband?"

"Not necessarily," she confided, "but it would have to be someone I feel strongly about."

"How strongly?"

"About the way I feel for you."

Dane drew in a deep breath, releasing it slowly with his words. "Something tells me, Jessi, that we should have brought along a chaperone."

"Chaperones went out of style decades ago," she reminded him.

"That's true. Thank goodness . . . I guess. Actually, I'm not—"

Jessi held up a hand, stilling his words. "Would you think I was being a tease if I said I wanted to wait for awhile?" she asked. "Despite my bold offer in the confines of that locked storage closet, I'm not ready for an intimate relationship." Hastily, she added, "with anyone."

"Not at all, Jessi. I'll respect whatever decision you make." Smiling at her, he amended, "Whatever decision *we* make."

Rockwood State Park was just as Dane had described it. Beautiful. Richly abundant with native flora and fauna, bursting with the fragrant aroma of pine trees, the park put Jessi's olfactory sensors in overdrive.

"It's so alive," she whispered. Her head tilted back, arms akimbo, she turned slowly around in a circle, taking in nature's bounty, one square inch at a time.

Acting the part of the well-informed tour guide, Dane told her, "The park houses over two hundred varieties of birds, over one hundred different species of plant, and nearly every indiginous forest animal known to man."

They hiked the intermediate trail in the morning, sharing a late morning snack of coffee, fruit and cheese next to an inland pond. Stretched out on a blanket, Jessi studied the clouds, her head pillowed on Dane's shoulder.

"Look," she said, pointing to a cloud formation, "can't you just picture a snowman, complete with top hat."

"There, look," Dane added, joining in the game. "A camel."

"I'm so glad you brought me here, Dane."

"So am I. It's one of my favorite places. I can't think of anyone I'd rather share it with."

Jessi closed her eyes, letting his admission slip past her defenses. "Dane?"

"Hmm," he mumbled.

"Do you think we'll be able to wait?"

"I'd like to think so. I'd like to think I know myself well enough that I could stop when I had to."

"You're obviously stronger than me. There's nothing I'd like more right now than to—"

"Jessi. Don't." Rolling onto his side, he pulled her into his arms and kissed her. "Just one kiss," he promised. Taking another, he told her, "we'll stop in a minute."

"Yes," Jessi agreed, her hands moving anxiously across his sweatshirt-clad chest. "In a minute."

In the afternoon, they joined a group of beginning climbers for a try at the smallest of the park's climbing trails. No special equipment was needed. Each steep incline was pegged, and marked clearly, with resting points along the way.

By six that evening, they were tired and hungry. Helping Jessi into the truck, Dane reached across her body and drew the seatbelt across her chest, clicking the locking mechanism into place. In retreat, his hand brushed her breast. The accidental touch was incendiary, setting fire to the kindling of her body.

Like the kisses they'd barely controlled, and the intimate brushes of body against body during their trail walk, Dane's touch was unnerving. Jessi ached all over with unquenched desire. If the tense expression on Dane's face was any indication, he was suffering just as much as she, if not more.

Dane climbed behind the wheel and buckled himself in. After he'd put the truck in gear and turned onto the highway, he took Jessi's hand in his and held it tightly.

"Jessi?"

"Yes," she said lazily, lethargy setting in fast.

"I've got to go away for a few days."

His words brought her instantly alert. Immediately wary. "Why? Where?"

"Don't worry, sweetheart, it's only a meeting of county sheriffs. We're getting together in Lansing for a couple of days to review some new equipment and procedures."

Jessi closed her eyes, and rested her head on the back of the seat. Suspended somewhere between dreamland and reality, she tossed fitfully, her dreams filled with Dane waving goodbye from the top of the Empire State Building.

Dane stopped the truck in Jessi's driveway. Releasing his seatbelt, he slid across the seat and placed a gentle and undemanding kiss on Jessi's cheek.

"I'll miss you," she confessed.

"Not nearly as much as I'll miss you."

They walked to the door hand in hand. He kissed her good night quickly and without emotion, knowing that if he initiated anything more, he'd never be able to let her go. Her return kiss was sweet. Chaste, as if she understood his need for simplicity. Although he couldn't help the sudden tightening of his body, he did his best to ignore it.

"I'll call you from Lansing," he told her.

"When will you be back?" she asked.

He'd told her at least five times in the last ten minutes, yet he couldn't deny how badly he wanted to stay one minute longer, even if it meant answering her questions over and over again.

When Jessi awoke the next morning, her first thoughts were of how long the week would seem without Dane. The obvious solution would be to keep busy. Between the activities program and the last chapter of her cookbook, Jessi mapped out her days to the limit, using anything and everything she could think of to ward off the fact that Dane was away.

Erline tapped at the window, letting herself in through the screen door. "Morning, Jessi."

"Good morning, Erline." Holding up the pot, she asked, "Coffee?"

"Sure thing, Jessi, dear. I'll never turn down your coffee. Or . . ." she hedged, ". . . one of your spicy muffins."

Jessi opened the door on her bread box and retrieved yesterday's cinnamon-apple muffins, chosing the largest one for her friend and a smaller one for herself.

When she'd finished eating, Erline asked, "You were out a little late last night, weren't you?"

Jessi stifled the urge to laugh at Erline's motherly concern, answering seriously, "Yes, I was. I went with Dane on a hike through Rockwood Park."

"Dane, hmm. Things are getting pretty serious, aren't they?"

"Yes, they are."

"According to Mabel, you two belong together."

"I'm glad people think so."

"Well Mabel and me do. No matter what happens, we're all for seeing you and Dane together."

"What do you mean, no matter what happens?"

Lowering her voice, she whispered, "According to Mabel, Dane's old girlfriend, Marilyn, is on her way back to Brant Mills. She's lost her fancy New York job, and gotten herself in trouble—if you know what I mean."

"Why's she coming here?" Jessi asked, her heart skipping first one beat, and then another.

Immediately, her imagination conjured up the worst possible scenario—that of Dane and his former lover reuniting. A cold chill raced through Jessi, playing tag with her ragged heartbeat, the game's progress interrupted by Erline's response.

"Her family's here, for one thing."

"And the *other thing?*" Jessi demanded, certain that there was more.

"According to Mabel, Sherlee Adler—Marilyn's mother— claims Marilyn's coming back to marry Dane."

"But—"

Erline gathered Jessi's hand in her own larger one, patting the back of her fingers consolingly. "Don't you worry, Jessi. No matter what Sherlee says, Dane won't do nothing he doesn't want to. Mark my words, he'll tell that little snippet to take a hike."

"Are you sure?"

"Sure, I'm sure."

Jessi cast a glance in Erline's direction and then wished she hadn't. An indecisive frown creased the older woman's brow. Stepping out onto the landing, Erline offered Jessi a smile that didn't quite reach her eyes.

"See you later, Jessi."

Jessi could do no more than nod her farewell. Shutting the door between herself and Erline, Jessi leaned against the frame, a limp rag doll on shakey legs. Like the first fall a gymnast takes from the balance beam, Jessi felt her stomach plummet and her head spin.

What would Dane think of Marilyn's return? she wondered. Did he already know? Was that why he seemed so distant when they'd kissed goodnight?

The cold chill she'd felt before was back, working its way into the very marrow of her bones. She hadn't wanted to fall in love. She certainly didn't want a broken heart.

Yet, if Dane were to reconcile with his ex-fiancée that would be exactly what she'd get.

Ten

Dane tucked a towel around his hips, letting the thick terry cloth soak up the last of the water from his skin. Reaching for the telephone, he dialed his office number, knowing Pike would be there already and getting set to give morning report.

On the third ring, his deputy answered, "Good morning, Brant Mills Sheriff's office, Deputy Pike speaking."

"Morning, Ed, it's me."

"Morning, Dane. How's it going in Lansing?"

"We're wrapping up today. I should be home by six. Anything special going on there?"

"No . . . nothing that can't wait til you get back."

Dane was instantly aware of the change in Ed's usually robust voice. "Are you sure?" Dane asked.

"Just gossip. You know how it is."

Dane felt a sudden clenching of his stomach muscles, intuition telling him that Pike wasn't referring to just any gossip. "Like what?" he demanded.

"It's only gossip, Dane, nothing important."

A second, stronger, spasm tightened Dane's gut. "What gossip? About who?"

"About you," Pike stated simply.

Dane's first thoughts were of Jessi. If anyone so much as dared to besmirch her good name, they'd have to answer to him personally. "Go on."

"It's about Marilyn actually. Seems she's on her way back home."

"Marilyn's coming home for a visit?" Dane asked.

"No. According to Sherlee, she's coming home to stay. Mabel seems to think she wants you back."

Dane's snort of disbelief preceeded his bitterly issued, "Fat chance. The only business I have with that woman is making sure she knows we're through."

"I'm glad to hear that, Dane," Pike admitted. "You know there's never been no love lost between me and that conniving witch. Ever since she hightailed it outta here without waiting for you, I've suspected she wasn't all she was cracked up to be. And . . ."

"And?" Dane prompted.

"And I'd hate to see Jessi hurt. Jessi's a nice lady. She deserves better than to be on the wrong end of this whole fiasco."

Dane's chuckle displaced his previously sour mood. "I don't suppose there's a chance Jessi's been spared this foul bit of gossip, is there?"

"Not likely, especially considering the rest of it."

Pressing his fingertips to his temple in an effort to calm a suddenly aching head, Dane asked, "the rest of it?" When Pike didn't answer, Dane coaxed, "Come on, Ed, spit it out."

"It seems—despite modern medical technology—Marilyn's got herself in trouble—if you know what I mean. Rumor has it, she's looking for a husband and a father for her baby, and she's set her cap for you."

Thunder rumbled off in the distance, drawing Jessi from a restless night's sleep. She'd no sooner sat up on the side of her bed when the telephone rang, it's jarring peal pushing away the last remnants of sleep.

"Hello?" Jessi greeted sleepily.

"Good morning, beautiful."

"Good morning, Dane."

"How's my favorite girl this morning?"

Pushing a handful of curls out of her face, Jessi reminded him, "I'm not a *girl,* Dane."

"I know that, but thinking of you as a woman only turns me on. Without you here, being turned on is a real bear."

Jessi knew she should have been flattered by the offhanded compliment. Yet, in the back of her mind, she couldn't help but wonder if Dane was aware of Marilyn's imminent reappearance in Brant Mills. Tentatively, she asked, "Was there something special you wanted this early in the morning, Dane?"

"Just to tell you that I miss you. And, that I'll be home tonight. I was hoping we could go out for supper."

"That would be nice. What time shall I expect you?"

"Seven—if that's not too late."

"No, seven's fine."

"I've got to go, Jess. They're starting the first seminar in five minutes."

"All right. Have a good day. Bye, Dane."

"Good-bye, sweetheart, I'll see you at seven."

Sweetheart. Jessi's heart did a little jig within her chest, tripping over itself. He'd called her sweetheart.

Surely he wouldn't have wasted the endearment if he had any intention of taking up with his old flame. The unwanted thought came and went, sent packing by Jessi's firm belief in her feelings for Dane, and in his for her.

See, her inner voice prompted, *this confidence thing isn't so hard to get used to. Is it?*

Harley was waiting for Jessi when she reached the school. "Good morning, Harley," Jessi greeted.

"Mornin' Miss Jessi," he called back. "I asked Mr. Sparks if I could stay in your class instead of going swimming. He said I'd have to get your permission."

"What does your father say? Doesn't he expect you to take part in all the activities?"

"He don't care, long as he knows where I'm at."

"Maybe I should call him," Jessi suggested.

"If you want, though I know he won't mind. He's busy working, and caring for Cissy."

"Cissy?"

"My little sister. She's two-and-a-half. Our mom left right after she was born. Me and Dad are raisin' her."

Jessi reached out and ruffled Harley's longish hair, noticing for the first time how badly it needed cutting. "How does he watch Cissy while you're here?"

"He puts her in her playpen right next to his workbench. Sometimes Mrs. Simpson comes in and takes her for awhile."

"It was very nice of your dad to let you come to activities when he could have probably used your help at home."

"Yeah," Harley agreed, "he's like that—always wanting me to have fun. Sometimes I feel kinda like I should be doing more around home, but he just chases me outta the house and tells me to go play with the guys."

Harley left moments later to join *the guys,* and Jessi followed his progress from one group of children to the next. He'd certainly come out of his shell since the program began. He was even talking to *dumb old girls,* as Spider Walker called them. Harley, she realized, had quickly accomplished what she'd suspected he would. He'd wound his way around her heart until there was no mistaking how much she cared for him. Like the other children, as well as the adults, she'd come to care for them all far more than she'd ever thought possible.

At lunchtime, Sally and Jessi sat beneath the big oak tree in the center of the school yard eating their sandwiches and drinking juice. For dessert they had cookies baked by Sally's class.

"It seems kind of ironic, doesn't it?" Sally asked.

"What does?"

"That I'm teaching the cooking class, and you're the cookbook author."

Jessi shrugged. "I'd rather have done the gymnastics anyway."

"You miss it, don't you?"

Jessi thought about glossing over the subject—letting Sally's question pass with the most minimal of answers. Yet, like the friendship she'd formed with Harley, the bond she'd made with Sally was just as strong. For once, she thought, it might be nice to openly confide in someone exactly how she felt.

"Sometimes, I guess. Although, I was the first to admit my career was over. It took longer for my mom and dad to accept."

"I take it they were upset."

"That's putting it mildly. They'd put a lot of time, and a lot of money, into my training."

"Surely they understood—"

"Oh my mom does—now. Until the day he died, my father still hadn't forgiven me for letting him down."

Before Sally could comment, Jessi lifted herself from the ground and brushed off the seat of her shorts. Offering a hand to her friend, she pulled Sally to her feet.

"If you ever need an ear—" Sally began.

Smiling, Jessi told her, "I know exactly where to find you." Softly, she added, "Thanks."

"You're welcome."

Dane climbed Jessi's stairs two at a time, anxious to wrap his arms around her. Anxious to tell her she had nothing to worry about. *Past* anxious to taste her lips and sink himself into the sweetness of her mouth. Just the thought of kissing her so thoroughly brought him instantly alert, every nerve ending in his body tingling with the need of Jessi. Despite what he'd promised, he wasn't sure if he could keep from seducing her into making love.

Of course you can. You're a strong man. A considerate man.

You know, Dane answered his conscience, I liked you better when you were on the other side.

Drawing a deep breath, Dane lifted his hand and tapped on Jessi's door. He was about to knock a second time when the door opened, and Jessi stood framed in her doorway.

God, but she's beautiful. So beautiful, in fact, he stood there like a lump on a log, unable to say anything—even the most innocent greeting.

"Hello there," she said softly. "Would you like to come in?"

He nodded, still too dumbfound to speak. Where had Jessi gone? he wondered. When had this femme fatale come to take her place?

He stepped into the kitchen, his gaze never leaving the woman before him. From the top of her silky red curls, to the white eyelet blouse that bared her creamy shoulders. Then, on to the miniscule white skirt that showed more leg than most pairs of shorts. And what legs they were, tanned to perfection and bare but for the bracelet circling her slim ankle.

"Is something the matter, Dane?" she asked, as innocent as a child.

"No, nothing a cold shower won't solve."

Turning around in a circle, her arms spread gracefully at her sides, she asked, "You like my new outfit? I bought it especially for tonight."

Dane reached behind his back and shut the door, the nod of his head his only indication of approval.

Jessi's eyes were wide with excitement. The knowledge that he was the one who excited her, excited him in return. As slowly as his anxious body would let him, he moved forward. The closer he came, the farther Jessi retreated. The shorter the distance between them, the harder his heart pounded, the faster his breath came.

When he had her backed all the way to the kitchen sink, he took one last step, then laid his hands on the counter, one on each side of her hips, enclosing her in his man-made cocoon.

"You bought that outfit for me?" he asked.

Jessi swallowed, and nodded. "Yes, just for you," she said softly, the four simple words filled with emotion.

"I like it," he admitted. "Very much."

"You do?" she asked.

Lowering his head, he nuzzled beneath the loose curls that hung past her shoulders, kissing a trail along her soft, silky, throat. When he reached her ear, he whispered, "Yes, Jessi, very, very, much. As a matter of fact, the only thing I'd like better is to see you out of it."

Her sharp intake of breath was his reward, along with the kiss he took. Just as he remembered, she tasted as sweet as wild strawberries, as mesmerizing as fine wine. When he slipped his tongue between her teeth, she met him there, eager to please.

He needed to let her go. *Soon. But not yet.*

Jessi's knees were about to embarrass her by giving way and dropping her to the kitchen floor. Dane's arms were like sentinels on either side of her, yet she didn't feel imprisoned. His kiss drove her crazy, yet she didn't feel incoherent. What she felt was aroused. More aroused than she'd ever been, and more willing to part with her virtue.

"Dane?"

"Hmm," he mumbled against her cheek.

"I've been thinking about what we said about waiting."

"And?"

"I . . ." Her words stalled, her thoughts interrupted by the weight of Dane's hands on her shoulders.

He slipped his fingertips beneath the lace trimmed edge of her blouse, easing it aside until the neckline hung loosely against her upper arms. Leaning forward, he pressed a hot, open-mouthed kiss to her bare shoulder, holding her close by anchoring his hands at her waist. When one hand slid upward to rest just beneath her breast, he returned to her mouth, staking out another claim to Jessi's heart.

Every emotion she'd ever felt—every desire—were magnified tenfold here within Dane's embrace. She was hot, she was cold, she was shy one minute, and bold the next. When Dane slipped his tongue inside her mouth one last time, she did something she'd never done before. She bit him. Nipped really. Just as he'd once done to her. And, as she had, he trembled.

"Sweetheart," he whispered, releasing her mouth and pulling in a reviving draft of air.

Drawing on all her strength, Jessi tried again, "Like I was saying, I—"

"No, Jessi," he said, lifting his head, meeting her gaze. "Not yet. I shouldn't have let it go this far. We decided to wait, and I really believe that was the right decision. Don't you?"

She nodded, unable to verbally contradict what only moment's before she'd decided she wanted.

"Good." Stepping back, he righted her blouse, then lowered his hands to his sides. "Let's get going. I'm starving."

On their way to Milton for supper, Dane stopped the truck to watch the sun set over Beaver Lake. The deserted lake-side setting would have made the perfect place to continue what they'd started in Jessi's kitchen, yet Dane only held her hand, and placed a single chaste kiss to her brow before pulling the truck back into gear and continuing on his way to Milton.

The restaurant Dane chose was in the middle of town, a small family-run Italian cafe featuring what Dane referred to as the best lasagna this side of Sicily. The owners, Vito and Anna Fiori, were obviously good friends of Dane's, and thought it their duty to sing the sheriff's praises to his date.

"That's quite a fan club you have there," Jessi pointed out over the spumoni ice cream Dane selected for dessert.

"They're good friends of my parents and have known me since I was a boy."

"They seem very nice."

"Vito thinks you are *bella.*"

"He does, does he?"

"Oh yes, I can see it in his eyes."

"What does Anna think of that?" Jessi asked.

"She understands it's Vito's way to admire the beautiful women. As long as he only admires. I, on the other hand, couldn't be as docile."

"Really?"

"Yes, really. When it comes to you, my beautiful Jessi, looking isn't the only thing I want to do."

Jessi lifted a spoonful of ice cream to her mouth, using the diversion to mask her suddenly rioting senses. Dane's huskily spoken admission sent new and exciting emotions rushing through her, settling quite heavily in the center of her chest.

"Jessi?"

"Yes."

"I think it's time we got out of here, don't you?"

Nodding, she waited for Dane to pull out her chair and then stood on shaky legs.

Dane paid the bill and then escorted her outside. Settling his hands on each side of her waist, he lifted her into the cab of the truck. When she reached for the seatbelt, he was there ahead of her, their hands meeting and joining. Dane leaned closer, pressing her hands into the seat, placing his lips over hers. Initiating a long, wet kiss.

Moments later, he clicked the seatbelt into place and closed the door between them.

They were halfway back to Brant Mills before either of them spoke. Finally, Dane brought up the subject Jessi had been dreading.

"I don't suppose it's news to you that my ex-fiancée is back in town."

"Erline mentioned something about her," Jessi admitted.

"I haven't seen her, but in a town the size of Brant Mills, it'll be unavoidable."

"Rumor has it," Jessi ventured boldly, "she's looking for a husband."

Dane chuckled, but the sound wasn't a jovial one. "I pity the poor fool she sets her sights on."

"Rumor also has it, you're that fool."

Reaching up, Dane drew a hand through his hair, then reached out and took hold of Jessi's fingertips, drawing them to his lips for a fleeting kiss.

"I guess it's time I told you the whole story."

Over the next half-hour, Dane related the story of his infatuation with the high-school homecoming queen, and his foolish attempts at holding onto her after she'd seen the big city. Almost to a word, his account matched the one Erline had given weeks before.

By the time they'd reached the Patterson's driveway, Dane had covered the part about Marilyn selling her engagement ring to set up housekeeping with another man.

"I don't blame you for being angry," Jessi consoled. "I'd have reacted the same way."

''There's nothing between Marilyn and me but bad feelings. So, in case you were worried, don't be.''

''I won't deny worrying. Erline says she's beautiful. I can't help but—''

Shaking his head, Dane pressed his fingertips to Jessi's lips, sealing in her admission of jealousy.

''I'm not stupid, Jessi. I don't have to be burned more than once to know not to play with fire.''

They sat there in silence for a few minutes longer before Jessi asked, ''Are you coming up for coffee?''

''I don't think so, Jess.''

''Why not? Don't you want—''

''Oh, I *want* all right, but not coffee.''

Jessi released her seatbelt and scooted across the seat. Laying her hands on Dane's chest, she gazed up into his eyes. ''What is it you do want, Dane?''

''You, Jessi. All of you.''

Eleven

Jessi strolled around the market, her basket overloaded with fresh fruit and vegetables. Stopping in front of the next booth, she stared down at the intricate pattern of a hooked rug. Despite the rug's beauty, she barely noticed the geometric design. All she saw was Dane. All she felt was Dane.

Over the past few days, he'd called twice a day. Their conversations had started off innocently enough, she supposed. Yet, by the time they'd finished, she'd been as aroused as if he'd been right there with her, making love to her. She wasn't sure how much longer they could hold out. She wasn't even sure that she wanted to wait.

She suspected that the tenuous control they had over their emotions was what had kept Dane away. The telephone was safe, he'd said. Well, today, he couldn't help but meet her face to face. Today, she'd get to see him up close. She'd get to touch. And, with any kind of luck, she'd get to taste.

Jessi shook herself out of her day dreams, and lifted her head to scan the crowd. On the other side of the booth, she saw a friendly face.

"Good morning, Harley." Jessi waved and called to the boy, yet her gaze was on the man at Harley's side. Tall, with long

shaggy hair the same color as Harley's, she guessed this was
Alex Masters—Harley's father.

Harley tugged on the man's arm and dragged him around
the stall. With less than a table width separating them, Jessi met
the man's gaze. The first thing she noticed were the disfiguring
scars on his forehead and cheeks. The second, was his friendly
smile.

"Morning, Miss Jessi," Harley greeted. "This is my dad."

"Good morning, Mr. Masters," Jessi said.

"Just Alex," he responded. "It's nice to finally meet you,
Jessi. Harley's told me a lot about you—and about your gymnastics class."

"He's a quick learner, and a pleasure to teach."

As Jessi spoke, Alex Masters's attention was drawn down-
ward by a tug on his hand to the little girl at his side. Jessi's
gaze followed. Hidden behind Alex's jean-clad leg, she peeked
out at Jessi, a timid smile showing off a wealth of dimples.

"This is my sister," Harley confirmed.

"Hello," Jessi said.

" 'lo", the child responded shyly.

"You must be Cissy."

"Yeth."

"It's nice to meet you, Cissy."

"Nice," Cissy repeated, tentatively touching Jessi's fingers.

Jessi ruffled the girl's blonde bangs, then stood to face Harley
and his dad. Alex's gaze, she noticed, was diverted to somewhere behind her. When she turned to see what had grabbed
his interest, the first thing she noticed was Dane. The second
was the woman at his side.

And, just as Alex Masters was doing, Jessi stared.

Dark brown hair hung half-way down the woman's back,
the slightly curled ends catching on the knit fabric of her
sweater. She was looking at Dane as if he were a picnic lunch,
and she the hungriest person on earth.

Jessi did her best to ignore Dane and the woman, striking
up a conversation with Alex regarding Harley's prowess with
gymnastics. Alex was attentive, and obviously proud of his
son. Yet, he too, seemed preoccupied with something other

than their conversation. Like her, his gaze kept wandering across the square.

"Excuse me, Ma'am," Alex said, suddenly, "but I've got to be going."

"Sure, I—"

Jessi never got to finish her thought before he strolled off toward Dane, Harley at his side and Cissy clinging tightly to his belt loops.

"Here comes company," Dane pointed out.

The woman who was once going to be his wife turned her head, sending her long mane of hair swaying in the breeze, brushing her back in a teasing maneuver he had long since learned to ignore.

"Where?" she asked. "Who?"

"Right here," a deep voice answered. "Surely you haven't forgotten your *old friend* Alex, have you?"

"No, of course not. How are you, Alex?"

"No complaints." Turning toward Dane, he asked, "How's it going, Dane?"

"Not bad," Dane answered rather absently, his gaze scanning the surrounding grounds.

"If you're looking for Jessi Trainor, she's over by Miss Walton's hooked rug booth."

Dane acknowledged Alex's help with a grin and a nod of his head. Tipping his hat in Marilyn's direction, Dane excused himself, "Now that Alex is here, I'm sure you're in good hands. If you'll excuse me, I'm late for a lunch date." To Alex he said, "I'll see you next week for that tune up."

"Sure thing, Dane. Tuesday."

His feet already in motion, Dane called back, "Yeah, Tuesday."

The closer Dane came, the harder Jessi's heart pounded. His gaze had captured hers time and again. Now, the nearer he got, the more she felt as if she were a fish being reeled in by an expert angler. Without even trying, she could feel the heat of Dane's body, smell his unique scent, taste the sweetness of his kiss. When he smiled, Jessi felt as if she were being bathed in a ray of sunshine, coaxed to life by the breath of the sweetest, gentlest, wind.

"Hello, pretty lady," he greeted.

Dane lifted his hand and laid his fingertips against her cheek. With no more than the subtle turn of his hand, he stroked her gently, setting her skin on fire, stoking her internal embers. The warmth she'd sensed before magnified itself until Jessi felt as if she would burst into flames at any moment.

"Hello, Dane," she answered back. The husky timber of her voice sounded strange, even to her, and she wondered where the unusual richness had come from.

"How about a sandwich and glass of lemonade?" he asked.

"Sounds good."

Jessi expected Dane to take her to the corner cafe, or to one of the Saturday stalls. Instead, he led her down mainstreet and toward his office. Once inside, he shut the door behind them with the heel of his boot. The lock had no sooner clicked into place, when he was reaching for her, drawing her into his arms, guiding her through the narrow hall until they stood inside his private office.

Shutting the office door, he turned the handle on the blinds and sealed out the rest of the world. "I've been wanting to hold you ever since I first saw you this morning," he confessed. "You look so beautiful in that sexy little sundress of yours, it was all I could do not to carry you off to some sequestered little hideaway and have my way with you."

Jessi wrapped her arms around Dane as well, holding him to her with the gentle pressure of her hands against his waist. "Is that so?" she asked. "You certainly didn't look lost for company. As a matter of fact—"

Dane lowered his head, cutting off her words with the firm pressure of his mouth, stealing her breath with the crafty delving of his tongue. Jessi thought to protest his interruption, and would have done so had it not been for the overwhelming sensations flowing through her, warming her from head to toe with Dane's sensual heat.

"Oh, Jessi," Dane whispered against her lips, "what you do to me."

"No more than you do to me, Dane."

He kissed her again. With the palms of his hands flat against her hips, he pulled her forward until there was no doubt as to what she did to him. At the first brush of his body, she gasped. In response, he delved deeper, sliding his tongue completely into her mouth, filling her with his taste.

Jessi was floating on air, her only anchor to reality the urgent press of Dane's body against hers. When he laid his hand against the curve of her breast, Jessi felt only a momentary flicker of panic, the fleeting reaction buried quickly, resolutely, beneath the feeling that this was right—that it was acceptable to be held like this by the man she loved.

"Jessi, Jessi, Jessi." Her name a whispered benediction, his warm breath bathed her lips, her cheeks. Still whispering her name, he nibbled on her earlobe, the sensitive slope of her throat.

"Dane," she called softly, "please don't stop."

"No, Jessi, not yet." Tugging aside one of the straps of her sundress with his teeth, he pressed his lips to her bare shoulder, nipping playfully, leaving lover's marks on her skin. In a voice that sent shivers down Jessi's back, he told her, "Not until I have to."

Dane wasn't sure how much more of this he could take. Yet, by the same token, he wasn't sure of his ability to stop. Jessi was so trusting, so genuinely innocent. He was positive she had no idea how close he was to the point of no return, how tentative his restraint.

He knew, for both their sakes, he should end the kiss, step away, and reclaim his quickly fleeing sanity. He should do whatever was necessary to protect Jessi's virtue. Drawing on some inner well of strength he didn't realize he possessed, he lifted his head.

That was his first mistake.

Her lips glistened with the remnants of their kisses, shining nearly as brightly as her eyes. With a groan, he kissed her again. And again.

He tried a second retreat. Raising his head, he stepped back, the limply hanging strap of her sundress drawing his gaze like a bee to a pollen-rich flower. With a shaky hand, he reached out to right the strap.

That was his second mistake.

Rather than raise the strap, he lowered it. The bodice of the dress fell away, exposing her creamy breast, its smooth-as-satin perfection a sharp contrast to the dark pebbled nipple at its center. He blinked. Once, twice, but couldn't look away.

Jessi, he realized, was as mesmerized as he. She stood stock-still, her hands clenched tightly at her sides, her breath coming in short, staccato puffs. He reached out, his hand hovering, yet not enclosing, her breast. Sensations warred within him. He wanted to touch her, taste her. Take her. Yet, somewhere, buried deep inside, he knew he'd not be able to stop. Having become so wrapped up in loving Jessi, he would end up coaxing her into something she wasn't ready to give; taking the innocence he'd sworn to preserve.

He drew back, putting a second, and then a third, inch between his hand and Jessi's breast. Just when he thought he'd broken the spell, Jessi reached out, captured his hand, and pressed it to her breast.

"Touch me," she commanded softly. "Just once. Let me have one small sample of what it's like to make love."

He curved his fingers around her breast, enclosing her completely in his palm. Squeezing her gently. His fingers tingled and burned, set on fire by the soft, smooth, surface of Jessi's skin. When she would have stepped closer, he turned her around until she faced away from him.

He leaned forward, pressing kisses to the nape of her neck, drawing a thin line on her shoulder with his tongue. All the while, he held her. One hand at her waist, his fingers spread wide to fan over her hip. In his other hand, he held her breast—the prize she'd offered of her own free will.

"Jessi, sweetheart," he whispered, "I've got to let you go. If I don't—"

"I know," she admitted. "I shouldn't have asked, but I've never . . ."

Her words trailed away and her breath caught when he rubbed his thumb across her nipple, urging the crest to life, drawing her gasp, making her quiver in his arms.

"Help me, Jessi," he pleaded, "help me stop."

With shaky hands, she lifted his touch from her body. Then she reached up and righted the front of her sundress, pushing the strap back into place with fingers that trembled. A moment later she took a step forward, putting distance between them, breaking the invisible silken thread that bound them together in passion.

Jessi laid her forehead against the wall in front of her. Her heart was pounding, and her legs were weak. "That was close," she whispered.

"Too close," Dane agreed.

She could sense how near he stood. She could feel the residual passion emanating from his body. If she took one step backward, she'd once again feel the power of his desire; the warmth of his embrace.

There'd be no going back. At that point, you'd have crossed the line.

As calmly as she could manage, Jessi suggested, "You'd better get back to the square. Someone's sure to notice your absence."

"Jessi—"

"Come on, Dane," she encouraged lightly. "Let's get that sandwich and lemonade you promised."

Jessi couldn't believe how close she'd come to begging Dane to make love to her—how close she'd come to giving away what she'd claimed to be withholding for marriage.

You're inconsistent.

I'm confused, she countered. *So very, very confused.*

"Here you go," Dane said, laying the sandwich on the table in front of her. "I'll go back and get our drinks."

Jessi watched him walk away, her gaze on the broad expanse

of his back, the narrow indentation of his waist, the firmly rounded curve of his buttocks. He was one sexy man. And, for the time being, he was hers.

How long will that last?

What do you mean?

How long do you think it'll be before he gets tired of playing the gentlemen?

"I—" Jessi was about to answer her conscience when Dane appeared.

"I, what?" he asked.

"I wanted to thank you for lunch."

"You're welcome."

Dane sat opposite Jessi, watching the late afternoon shoppers browsing for last minute bargains. On the far side of the square, vegetables were being marked down for quick sale. Friendly banter permeated the air, filling Dane's thoughts with how wonderful it felt to live in a such a peaceful, caring town. He also thought of Jessi, and of how badly he wanted her to forget her traveling plans—forget her dreams for life in the big city— and stay here with him.

How had he ever thought he could live without her? Why had he fought the idea of a relationship with Jessi in the first place? All his original theories about why he wasn't right for her, or she for him, had been pushed aside by a desire he could no longer control; a thirst he could no longer quench. If only he could find the right words, and the right time, to tell her how he felt.

What was wrong with today in your office?

No. It's got to be somewhere perfect. The words have to come first, before the kissing and petting. I don't want her to think I'm only saying the words to get what I want.

How about at the picnic?

How about minding your own business?

Jessi brushed her hair, stroke after stroke after stroke, until the wild red strands crackled with static electricity. The sparks that emanated from her hair reminded her of the sensual electricity she'd experienced while being held in Dane's arms. Her reflection in the dressing table mirror told her she hadn't yet forgotten how far they'd gone, how close she'd come to embarrassing herself by asking for something he wasn't prepared to give.

Maybe if he knew you were in love with him he'd change his mind. Or, maybe he'd turn tail and run. Like the old saying goes, 'Once burned, twice shy.'

She closed her eyes, letting all Dane had said, all Dane had done, replay itself in her mind. Her lips tingled with the memory of Dane's kiss. Her breathing accelerated, sent into an uneven rhythm by the thoughts of Dane's touch. She felt her body change. Soften. Heat gathered in her very center, radiating out until every limb was warm, every inch of her exposed skin flushed.

She pressed her hand to the valley between her breasts and drew in a deep measure of air. Beneath her flattened palm and spread fingers, her heartbeat raced. Was this what passion did to you? Was this how love made you feel? Restless? Dissatisfied?

Satisfaction, she realized now, would come only when she and Dane made love.

Twelve

Jessi stared out the window overlooking the school's parking lot. All the children were gone. Ed Pike had dropped off the last of the swimmers over an hour ago. All the volunteers had left shortly thereafter. She was well and truly alone.

Dragging the balance beam into place, Jessi slipped out of her canvas runners and flexed her toes. Although she knew it was only her imagination, the soles of her feet seemed to tingle in anticipation. In an unconscious movement, she picked up the rosen bag and tossed it from one hand to the other. When the tossing became repetitive, she stared down at her hands and mentally noted her nervousness.

She had known this day would come.

It was as inevitible as loving Dane Logan.

Today, she intended to challenge the eight-foot wooden beam—to lift herself four-feet off the floor and face her hidden fears.

The minor challenge she'd met the day the beams were delivered was nothing compared to this. Then, during the second week of class, she'd bravely stepped up on the lower beam. For the first time in six years, she'd put herself on the line for an audience. There'd been a single moment of panic, when her bare feet had first met the smooth surface of the wood, and she'd wondered if even such a small adversary could defeat her. Barely six inches off the floor, she'd swallowed her fear and demonstrated the proper techniques the students would need to master the beam. The trust she'd seen in the children's eyes had coaxed her along and given her strength.

Jessi closed her eyes and drew a deep, steadying breath. Although her palms were damp with perspiration, she reached out and gripped the beam. Hoisting herself up, she sat astride the wood, one leg dangling to the side, the other leg bent, her foot pressed flat against the beam in front of her.

That's it, Jess. See how easy that was? Now, lift yourself up and get started.

Despite the urging of her well-intentioned conscience, try as she might, she couldn't bring herself to make that final effort; to boost herself up one more notch. Twice, she braced her arms and lifted. Both times, she sank back in defeat.

Jessi, her conscience scolded, *don't back out on me now. Don't let this stupid piece of lumber keep you from reclaiming your peace of mind.*

"I won't" she whispered to herself, "just give me a minute."

Placing her hands on the narrow strip of wood, Jessi raised herself up a third time until, finally, she stood on the beam. Her legs felt like rubber, her knees wobbled, yet still she stood—her back straight, her shoulders squared, her chin up and her head held high. She drew another deep breath to calm her fluttering heartbeat, and said a silent prayer for strength.

You've done it, Jess. Really done it!

Her gathered breath came out on a sigh of relief, accepting the silent congratulations of her conscience. Now, if she could only make it to the end of the beam, she could conquer this emotional albatross. She false-started once, twice, a third time.

Tentatively, she took the first step. As she inched forward, she told herself that, even if she fell, there was no chance of sustaining physical injury. If anything, the pain she suffered would be mental. Jessi pushed the possibility aside, choosing instead to concentrate on more important thoughts.

She thought of Dane, and of how much he'd come to mean

to her in such a short period of time. The memory of his kisses boosted her confidence another notch, coaxing her into taking a second step, and then a third.

She thought back about all she'd accomplished since coming to Brant Mills, and of all the friends she'd made. She thought of how much she'd grown, both as a woman and as a person. Spurred on by thoughts of her small victories, she took another step.

Suddenly, her foot slipped and she slid forward. Arms stretched out for balance, she righted herself and closed her stance. The heart that had only fluttered before now pounded a distinct rhythm in her chest.

When she thought she might flee the beam in terror, her inner-voice encouraged her. *Come on, Jess, keep going. It's only a few more feet.*

Swallowing her fears, she tried again. The more steps she took, the more familiar the wood felt beneath her feet. Stopping just short of her goal, she glanced back over her shoulder to see how far she'd come. Seven feet. Not that great a distance in some ways—yet monumental in others.

Rather than take those two final steps, Jessi lowered herself to the beam, stretching out until she could lay back and stare up at the ceiling. She bent one knee and anchored her foot to the beam, balancing herself by nothing more than the even distribution of her weight. Closing her eyes, she collected her thoughts and planned the two or three exercises she would try.

Dane stood off to the side, safely hidden behind the half-closed gym door. He should speak up, he realized. Yet the sight of Jessi, as she fought a silent battle with the balance beam, had reeled him in on an emotional level like none he'd ever known. Just the sight of her boosting herself upward lifted his heart to new heights and filled his throat with a lump he couldn't quite swallow.

When she'd slipped, it had been all he could do to keep from rushing forward to offer a steadying hand. She'd regained her balance, and he'd felt as proud as if he'd been the one to help her stand.

After reaching the opposite end of the beam, she'd looked back over her shoulder and he'd seen her excitement, her satisfaction in her accomplishment. In that one fleeting moment, he'd realized how much he loved her, and how badly he wanted to ask her to be his wife.

He'd been on the verge of stepping out of the shadows and voicing his request when she'd leaned forward. Slowly, she'd bent and twisted her small frame like a cat curling up for an afternoon nap. By the time she'd finished her unconsciously sensuous moves, she was stretched out on the beam, one arm above her head, one knee bent for leverage. Her shoulders fell back to either side of the beam, pushing her small breasts upward against her t-shirt. Despite the clenching of his fists, Dane's palms itched with the urge to enclose her, caress her, arouse her.

As he watched, she sat up and grasped the wood on each side of her hips. Lifting herself skyward with no more than the strength of her arms, she landed effortlessly on her feet in the center of the beam. He swallowed, the lump in his throat growing bigger, the racing of his pulse accelerating until he could feel it beating against every point of contact in his body.

Jessi moved again, executing a perfect turn until she faced toward him. The broad grin she wore drew his own smile. The glide of her tongue across her full lower lip drew his soft groan. The thought of kissing Jessi, and tasting her enticing flavor, became first and and foremost in his mind.

Yet, when he meant to step forward, something stopped him. Something told him she wouldn't want to be disturbed. This was her private time. A time of self-discovery. Of triumph. He turned and started to walk away, stopping only long enough to steal one last glance at the smiling woman on the homemade balance beam.

Dane slipped behind the wheel of the patrol car. Moments later, he was on the highway and headed out of town. He wanted to go to Jessi. He wanted to confess his feelings. Yet, here he was, stuck working the three-til-midnight shift as a favor to Deputy Stiles.

Most times he didn't mind the afternoon shift. Tonight he did. Tonight he wanted to be with Jessi. He wanted to tell her he'd watched while she'd defeated her fears. He wanted to make slow, passionate love to her to the point where stopping was only a remote possibility. He wanted to tell her how he felt about her, and ask her to marry him. Unfortunately, his wants would have to wait—at least for another few hours.

Driving along Mapleridge, Dane slowed down opposite the park. A favorite place for teenagers on a warm, starlit night, he mentally cataloged each and every car along the two block stretch of parking lot. At the end of the row was Marilyn's car, with Marilyn sitting cross-legged on the hood. Her head was thrown back, her arms supporting her slender frame. Even from this short distance, she looked almost human—almost approachable. Perhaps, Dane noted rather unwillingly, impending motherhood had softened her hard edges.

He pulled into the spot next to hers and climbed out of the car. Seconds later, he stood at her side. "Evening, Marilyn."

"Hi, Dane. Lovely night, isn't it?"

"Yes," he agreed. "What brings you into town alone?"

She chuckled, yet the sound held no humor. "How else would I be? I didn't exactly come back with husband-in-tow, did I?"

"No, I guess not."

"Besides, I kinda like it this way. Not having to cater to anyone but myself."

"What about the baby? You'll have to cater an awful lot then."

"I know. Maybe that's why I'm enjoying the solitude so much right now."

"Bull," he stated firmly. "This isn't some stranger you're talking to—it's me. You never liked being alone, and you know it. If you'd have been content being alone—even for a week or two—you would have waited for me. You'd have been able to do without company."

"That's not—"

Angrily, Dane cut her off, "Don't even try denying it. I was there. Remember? One day too early. Hell, that poor guy couldn't get out of the apartment fast enough."

Marilyn laughed, and this time the sound had more of an honest ring to it. "What did you expect, Sheriff? The look on your face was enough to scare a rabid grizzly bear. That Manhattan stockbroker never stood a chance."

Dane laughed as well, caught up in the memory of the red-faced man fleeing the bedroom, and then the apartment, half-dressed and dragging his fancy silk suit behind him.

"I take it," Dane said, "that the fellow you refer to as 'that Manhattan stockbroker' isn't the father of your baby."

She shook her head but didn't speak.

"What was he then? Just on one-night-stand?"

"Yes. One of many."

Dane gave a snort of disgust, then spun on his heel, intent on leaving before he said something he'd surely regret.

"Don't go, Dane," she called out. "Please. Not yet."

"Listen, Marilyn, there's something you should know."

"What? That you have a girlfriend?" He nodded but, before he could speak, she went on, "Her name's Jessi, right?"

"Yes."

"According to Harley, she walks on water."

"Most likely only in his eyes . . . and mine."

"Are you in love with her?"

He thought about answering in the affirmative, but said instead, "That's between Jessi and me."

"You haven't told her yet, have you? You never were one for revealing your feelings."

"My life's my own."

She shook her head, and reminded him, "Even when we were engaged, you never really opened up. It was almost as if you were hiding a secret. If I hadn't known you since we were fifteen, I'd have thought you had a shady past."

"I guess, somewhere deep inside, I knew we weren't right for each other. Maybe that's why I never opened up. You hated this small town. I loved it. You wanted bright lights." Nodding toward her car, he added, "And BMW's. I wanted walks in the warm summer moonlight and an old, but reliable truck."

Reaching up, she laid a soft hand against his cheek, and asked, "You remember what else you wanted that we couldn't agree on?"

Dane took hold of her caressing hand and placed it back at her side. Nodding, he confessed, "Yes, I remember."

"Well," she said, sighing and patting her still-flat stomach, "looks like I beat you to it."

"Yeah, I guess you did."

Dane stared out over the small pond, seeing not the water, or the few geese nibbling at the milkgrass at water's edge, but the past. His and Marilyn's past. And, like their relationship had done years before, his memories sank into the murky water, taking with it all his leftover feelings—both good and bad, leaving him indifferent.

"How's things going with you and Alex?"

"Alex?" she asked.

"According to your mother, you've been seeing a lot of him lately."

"He always was fun. Remember the time—I think it was ninth grade—when he put the frog in Miss McCandless's briefcase. She screemed so loud, I was sure she was going to shatter a window."

"He didn't do that," Dane corrected.

"Sure he did. I remember—"

"I did it."

"You did it?" she repeated in disbelief.

"Yep—on a dare."

"But Alex took the blame. He got suspended for two days."

"He sure did. He went fishing both days. I never forgave him for that. Those should have been my trout."

"His kids are great. Harley's such a bright boy, and little Cissy's so adorable."

"He's a good father," Dane pointed out. "He's a good man, period. Problem is, he's lost faith in himself. Since the accident, he sees himself as ugly, both inside and out."

"That's not true," she defended.

Dane nodded his agreement, then said softly, "You're telling the wrong guy. I'm not the one you've got to convince."

Pulling out onto the highway, Dane made one last pass on the outskirts of town before turning down Highgait Lane. Restlessness, egged him on. *Two more hours. How would he last two more hours without seeing Jessi?*

He wouldn't. He had to see her now.

That thought in mind, he turned left at the next intersection and onto Elmwood. The lights in Jessi's apartment were still on even though it was nearly eleven. He parked the patrol car in the driveway and tiptoed up the stairs.

He could see her through the window, sitting at the table, a mug of something steamy clutched in her hands. She was wearing her bathrobe and her hair was hanging loose around her shoulders.

This isn't a good idea. Turn around while you still can. Contrary to his conscience's advice, he lifted his hand and tapped on the door.

Jessi parted the curtains and stared out into the dark night. A moment later, she opened the door. "Hello, Dane," she greeted. "What brings you here this late at night?"

"Can I come in?"

"Of course."

Rather than draw her into his arms like he wanted, he paced the length and width of the kitchen, choosing his words carefully.

"Is something wrong, Dane?" she asked.

"No, sweetheart. Nothing's wrong."

"Are you still on duty?"

"Yeah, for another two hours." He made a second, broader sweep of the room, then said, "Listen, Jessi, there's something I think you should know."

Here it comes. He's through with little-girl games. He's tired of waiting. More bravely than she felt, she asked, "Yes, Dane, what is it?"

"I had a long talk with Marilyn earlier tonight."

A chill raced unchecked up Jessi's arms. "What about?"

"We came to terms with our past, mostly."

"You don't have to tell me this . . . I mean . . . it's not any of my business."

"I know how people in this town talk. Someone undoubtably saw us talking, and I didn't want you to hear about it second hand."

"That's good of you, but I don't see—"

"Jessi," he responded firmly. "I was only wishing her luck. Nothing more."

Jessi's heart lifted, and she asked, "She's leaving?"

"No, she's staying right here. And, she's set her sights on Alex Masters. She seems to think she can heal his emotional wounds."

"What do you think?" she asked.

"Anything's possible, I suppose. The Marilyn I broke up with wouldn't have stood a chance. She was spoiled and willful. But, now, she seems different. Maybe she's ready to settle down." At the first sight of worry on Jessi's face, he added quickly, "just not with me. I've got my sights set on someone else."

"Really?"

Pressing her hand to his lips, Dane bit gently at the base of her thumb, then drew his tongue across the indentations made by his teeth. Jessi shivered, and he drew her into his arms.

"Yes," he whispered just prior to claiming her mouth, "really."

His kiss was warm, sweet, magical, setting the nerve endings in her body alive with electricity. Were Dane not holding her firmly in his embrace, she would have floated to the ceiling like a renegade helium balloon. Had she not felt the heavy press of Dane's solid body against her own, she might have thought she was dreaming. Like her dreams of late, the sensations she felt were both exciting and frightening.

Slowly, Dane lifted his head. His eyes were glazed over with desire. His upper lip glistened with perspiration. Lifting herself onto her toes, Jessi bravely licked away the tiny droplets with the tip of her tongue. Dane's growl of satisfaction was like a symphony to her ears.

The thought that she could arouse him half as easily as he

aroused her was terribly exciting. Teasingly, she asked, "This someone else wouldn't happen to be anyone I know would it?"

He chuckled, but didn't answer. Instead, he grazed her cheeks, her chin, the slope of her throat with his fingertips. Like the tingles she'd felt before, her body came alive, heating to his touch, burning where he lingered.

With one hand, he loosened the belt of her robe. With the other, he swept the neckline open and back until it hung precariously around her shoulders and sagged open in the front. Her nightgown, though modestly cut, did little to hide the flushed skin beneath.

She swallowed, yet couldn't speak. Dane was staring at her, his gaze caressing her face, her throat, her bare shoulders, much the same as his fingertips had done. When his eyes reached the scoop neckline of her gown, they lit with a fire Jessi had never seen before—a fire so bright, and so openly honest, that it was all she could do to keep from lifting her hands and shielding herself from his gaze.

"Dane, I—" she began, only to let the words die away when he lifted his hand and traced the swell of her breast with his fingertips. Her breath came out on a ragged rush, only to be caught again when he repeated the caress.

Less than a heartbeat later, he was righting her robe and tightening the belt at her waist. "I can't stay here, Jessi. Not like this. I thought I could just come by and see you, tell you how I feel, but I—"

"How you feel?" she asked. Hope welled up from within. Her pulse raced in anticipation of the words she longed to hear.

"How I've felt since the first day I met you. When you started relaying your story about the flasher, all I could think of was how beautiful your hair was, how beautiful you were, and how badly I wanted to kiss you."

"You mean you never even heard a word of my report?"

"I heard every word. Your voice enthralled me. I couldn't believe such a husky, sexy voice could come out of so small a package."

"You think my voice is sexy?" she asked in disbelief.

"So much so that I was hoping the jerk would show up again, just so you'd have a reason to call me. I wanted to see you again, as soon as possible."

"Well, you certainly got your chance. Unfortunately, it wasn't under the best of circumstances."

"Oh, I don't know. You looked pretty damn enticing soaking wet."

"I looked ridiculous. I—"

Jessi's claim was interrupted by the two-way radio Dane had set on the kitchen counter beside him.

"Unit eleven, come in please," came the annonymous voice.

Dane lifted the radio and said, "this is eleven, over."

"Unit eleven, we have a report of a MVA on Interstate Two, five miles out of town. Over."

"Any injuries reported?"

"Nothing serious. Over."

Glancing at his watch, he confirmed, "Unit eleven responding at twenty-one ten. Over."

"Ten-four, unit eleven. Be advised, the driver of the second car is allegedly passed out. Over."

"I'm on my way. Alert an ambulance to meet me there. Over."

"Roger, unit eleven."

Before he could say anything, Jessi had the door open.

He gave her a light peck on the cheek and stepped out onto the porch. "Listen, Jessi, I—"

"Go," Jessi urged.

He stepped down two steps, then turned back, "Jessi, I—"

Jessi's heart did a flip-flop in her chest. He looked so intent. His eyes had a different glaze about them now—one of seriousness, rather than passion. Encouragingly, she prompted, "Yes, Dane?"

"I . . . I gotta go, Jessi. I'll call you tomorrow."

Thirteen

Tuesday and Wednesday flew by, driven by the children's enthusiasm toward both their activities program and the upcoming holiday. Jessi felt overwhelmed at times by the outpouring of friendship she received from people who, only a few months before, were total strangers. Nearly half the town had invited her to be their guest at the Fourth of July picnic. As graciously as possible, she'd told them she already had plans, but hoped she'd see them there.

"There'll be fireworks, Miss Jessi," Harley pointed out for the tenth or twelfth time in the past hour.

"Don't forget our part in the festivities," Jessi reminded him.

"I can't wait to see my Dad's face when I show him what I've learned so far."

"Me too," a young girl said excitedly. "Wait'll they see me on the balance beam."

"How 'bout you, Miss Jessi? Are you going to give a demonstration?" Harley asked. "I heard my dad and Miss Mabel at the store talking 'bout how you was going to be in the Olympics."

Jessi shook her head. "No, Harley, I'm leaving the showing off to you kids."

"Come on, Miss Jessi," another child encouraged, "at least show us what you learned getting ready for the 'lympics.'"

Jessi glanced around her corner of the gymnasium, taking in each smiling face, each hopeful expression. It was on her lips to refuse but, for some reason she never quite understood, she said, "Okay, but only one or two exercises."

Together she, Harley and the Martin twins put the equipment in place. The children sat in a circle around the large balance beam, leaning back on their hands to get a better view. Half-eaten lunches were quickly forgotten when Jessi slipped off her shoes and picked up the rosen bag. As she'd shown the children to do, she dusted her hands with the chalky compound.

Boosting herself up onto the beam, Jessi took a moment to gather her composure. Somewhere off in the distance, she heard the faint sounds of music and realized that one of the children must have turned on the tape player she often used during class time. She let the music guide her, moving in perfect orchestration with its gentle beat.

One by one, the others gathered. Dane stood off to the side and watched them come. Students from other classes filtered in first, followed by the other teachers, and then the volunteers. No one said a word, but stood enthralled by the lovely young woman on the balance beam, her body flowing to a distinct rhythm that belonged to her alone.

As he had when he'd watched her other attempt at the beam, Dane absorbed every move she made, every step she took, every bend and twist of her body. She seemed oblivious of the crowd around her, performing more for herself than any panel of would-be judges.

Less than five minutes later, she dismounted with a twisting turn, landing firmly on the mat beside her. She winced once, the small quirk of her facial muscles barely discernable, and most likely missed by everyone but Dane himself.

Thunderous applause greeted her dismount. Gracefully, she turned and faced the gathered audience. With precise movements, she lifted her hand above her head and saluted the crowd just as she had once saluted world-class judges. Before she could step off the mat, the children were swarming around her like bees around a honeycomb, each one buzzing louder than the next with their praise.

One by one, as they had come, the people dispersed, leaving only Jessi and her class in the corner of the gym. While the children gathered the remnants of their lunches, Dane stepped forward.

"Very nice, Jess. Very nice, indeed."

"Thank you."

"Is your knee okay?"

She glanced down at the floor, then met his gaze. "How'd you know?"

"There's not much about you that escapes my attention."

"Really?" she asked, her expression one of sincere surprise.

"Yes, really. Especially if its a frown, or a grimace, altering your otherwise perfect features."

Jessi shook her head in disagreement, telling him, "there's absolutely nothing perfect about me."

Mindful of the pint-sized audience surrounding them, he briefly touched her hand. "To me, Jessi, you're perfect."

The urge to stroke the pink satin finish that had suddenly appeared on her cheeks made him clench his hands at his sides. "Shall I pick you up for the festivities tomorrow, or are you riding with Erline and Abel?"

"I think I'll walk. The weather's supposed to be perfect."

"I'll drive you home."

"If I remember correctly, you promised me a drive to Crescent Bay."

He wagged his eyebrows in mock lechery, and teased, "Only if you promise to behave yourself."

Shaking her head, she confided, "I never make promises I can't keep."

The holiday hadn't come fast enough to suit Jessi. If the truth be known, she was as excited about the picnic, the games, and the fireworks, as any one of her students. It was a beautiful, sun-drenched day. A perfect day. A day made especially for long walks and serious talks. The right day to admit she had a change of heart, an alteration of what was once her dream.

Stepping out into the bright sunlight, she pulled her straw hat down to shade her eyes and lifted her picnic basket onto her arm. When she turned off of Elmwood and onto Highgate Lane, Dane was there to meet her.

"Has anyone ever told you, with that basket on your arm, you resemble Little Red Riding Hood?"

She smothered a giggle behind her hand, and glanced down at her pink shorts and pink-and-white stripped halter top. "No, I can't say as they have."

"Would you believe I'm the friendly woodsman and I'm here to protect you?"

This time, she laughed out loud. "No, but I might believe you're the big, bad wolf."

Dane pressed a hand to his heart, feigning great despair. "Not I, fair Riding Hood. You must have me mistaken for someone else."

Jessi placed her hand in his offered one, and gave him her basket. "We'll see about that, Mr. Wolf, won't we?"

The day's activities ran smoothly, the games drawing the town's children, along with a proudly enthusiastic group of parents. Jessi, Dane noted, played along with the children, helping out with the games, offering herself as a partner for the mother and daughter balloon race in place of a visibly pregnant mom. Just as he had, Brant Mills was falling in love with Jessi.

Later in the afternoon, the two of them sat beneath a big oak and shared a large slice of watermelon.

"You're really into this, aren't you?" Dane asked.

"I haven't had this much fun in ages. If ever."

"Didn't you have picnics like this when you were a kid?"

"No, at least not that I remember. About all I remember of my childhood was mats and beams and practice. And coaches and trainers, and more practice. I'd never even been to the circus until I turned eighteen. From the time I was four, up until I couldn't compete anymore, it was always work, Jessi, work; smile, Jessi, smile. Practice, Jessi, practice."

"Doesn't sound like much of a childhood," he commented.

"Actually, I didn't mind. But, then again, I had no idea what I was missing."

"What about your brother? Was he as actively involved in gymnastics as you were?"

"Steve?" She laughed and shook her head. "Steve was a bookworm. A do-gooder. All he ever wanted to do was save the world from starvation."

"I take it that's why he became a social worker."

"Yes, and he's one of the best." Sighing, she added, "I really miss him."

"Not so much that you want to leave Brant Mills, I hope."

"No. Karen was right. You were right. This is a wonderful town, with friendly, caring people. I think I've finally found a home, one I'd probably never find in a big city. Now all I have to do is find myself a permanent place to live. I can't stay above Abel and Erline's forever."

"No, I don't guess you can. Although, available houses are few and far between in Brant Mills. You might just have to share."

"Share?"

"Yes, as in—"

"Miss Jessi, Miss Jessi." Harley's urgent call interrupted Dane's words. "Hurray, Miss Jessi. It's time for the gymnastics demonstrations."

Dane sprang to his feet and offered Jessi his hand. "Come on, Miss Jessi," he teased, "you don't want to miss out on the fun."

In turn, each child showed off what they'd learned, either on the balance beam, the mat, or the pommel horse. Harley's precision moves drew gasps and claps from the crowd, along with Alex's proud grin. Held firmly on Alex's hip, little Cissy struggled to keep her eyes open.

At the end of the demonstrations, Mayor Byrne made a short speech thanking each of the volunteers for their efforts with the first summer program. When the crowd cleared only Dane, Jessi, Alex and Marilyn were left standing in the center of the field.

"Jessi," Dane said firmly, "this is Marilyn. Marilyn, this is Jessi."

Marilyn offered her hand. "It's nice to finally meet the woman I've heard so much about. Harley sings your praises, as does half the town."

"I'm very flattered that they think so much of me," Jessi confessed.

It seemed to Jessi that both Dane and Alex were holding their breath. Were they as unsure of Marilyn as she was? Jessi wondered.

As if she could read all their minds, Marilyn took Jessi's arm and drew her away from the men. In low, hushed tones, she confided, "You know, Jessi, I should be terribly jealous."

"You should?"

"Yes. You have a hold on Dane, I never had. Not once, in all the years we dated, did he ever look at me with such longing in his eyes. When I first came back here, it was to try and win Dane back. I see now that I don't stand a chance."

"I'm sorry, I—"

"Don't be sorry, Jessi. Dane deserves someone like you."

"Someone like me?"

"Yes. You're sweet. You care about this town, and its people—probably as much as Dane does. I'm not sure I'll ever be truly happy here. Still, Alex seems to think he can change my mind about small town living."

"Are you going to give him the chance?" Jessi asked.

"Why not? I've nothing else planned for the next six months except bloating up like a balloon. It'll be interesting to see if he's as eager when I look like a blimp."

By the time their conversation was finished, they'd completed the circle around the picnic tables and come to a halt right where they'd started, arriving at the tail end of Dane's and Alex's discussion of the upcoming Detroit Tiger and Toronto Blue Jays series.

"Ready?" Alex asked, his gaze lingering on Marilyn's smiling face.

"Are you leaving so soon?" Jessi asked.

Alex nodded. "Cissy's sound asleep, and I've got some work to do."

"What about the fireworks later tonight?" Dane asked.

"We'll be back about nine-thirty. My name would be mud if these two missed the big celebration."

"Harley could stay with us," Dane suggested.

"Thanks anyway, Dane, but he has some chores to do, too."

"We'll save a spot for you by the fountain," Jessi offered.

"Great," Alex acknowledged, "we'll meet you there."

The afternoon's activities winding down, Jessi and Dane grabbed a few minutes peace and quiet beneath a willow tree. Sitting side by side, they watched as the families around them began setting out more food and preparing for their evening meal.

"So?" Dane asked, drawing Jessi from her perusal of a nearby group, "what'd you and Marilyn talk about?"

"You mostly."

"Me?"

"Yes, you. She admitted coming back to town with the intention of reconciling with you."

"Did she also tell you that I set her straight on that idea right away?"

"Not in so many words, but she did say that she realized she didn't stand a chance."

"She never lacked for brains, I'll give her that."

"Do you think she and Alex might get together?"

Dane shrugged, and admitted, "I'm not sure. They're certainly opposite personalities."

"They say opposites attract."

"I don't know about that. We're not opposites, yet we're certainly attracted to one another."

"Well, I suppose there's always an exception to every rule."

"I'd like to think you and I will always be the exception, Jess. And that we'll always feel this way."

"What way is that, Dane?"

Stretching out on the plaid blanket beneath them, Dane laid his head in Jessi's lap. "Like every time we touch we short circuit our common sense."

"You feel that way too?" she asked, her amazement evident in her voice.

"All the time."

"I thought it was just me."

"Is that the way I make you feel, Jess?"

Reaching out, she stroked a lock of hair from his forehead and nodded. "Yes. Sometimes, when you kiss me, I don't know which end is up. You unravel me so quickly, I can't seem to catch my breath."

"How much longer do you think we'll be able to hold out without making love?"

"I'm not sure I'll make it through the night," she confessed. "How about you?"

"Hell, I'm not even sure of the next twenty minutes."

Dane and Jessi made the rounds from one family table to the next, accepting a bite of this, a helping of that. By the time they'd reached the table they shared with the Patterson's Jessi felt as if she was about ready to burst.

"I can't believe how much I've eaten," Jessi admitted.

"I know just how you feel," Erline agreed, "I've been eatin' all day. So's Abel."

"Where is Abel?" Jessi asked.

"Over there under the tree sleeping off his third helping of your lemon cream pie. He claims its the best pie he ever ate."

"Amen," Dane added, patting his stomach for emphasis. "I ate just as many pieces as Abel did—if not more."

Jessi turned full circle, taking in the groups of people around them. "It seems as if everyone's overdone it. Everywhere you look, someone's napping. Even the children seem to be winding down."

"They'll perk back up when it gets dark," Dane told her. "Nothing excites them quite like the fireworks."

Erline agreed. "That's for sure. Why, I remember—"

Erline's memories were cut short by Harley's frantic call. "Sheriff Logan! Sheriff Logan! Come quick!"

"What is it, Harley?" Dane asked, bending down on one knee to meet the boy's tearful gaze.

"Something awful's happened. It's Cissy. Come quick. Please."

Dane grabed Harley's hand and ran full speed toward his truck, Jessi close on his heels. Ed Pike met Dane at the road.

"What's happened?" Ed asked.

"I'm not sure. Can you tell us more, Harley? What's happened to Cissy?"

Between gasps of air, Harley managed, "She's fallen in the old well hole."

Dane lifted Harley into the truck. Jessi climbed into the other side. "Light 'em up, Ed," Dane shouted, "and lead the way."

Lights flashing and sirens blaring, the patrol car sped out of town and toward the abandoned well.

They pulled into Alex's long driveway, the patrol car, then Dane's truck, followed by a car carrying two deputies and the volunteer fire chief. Dane and Jessi followed Harley's lead, winding their way down an old beaten path to the back of the property. Ed and the others followed in their wake.

When they arrived at the well, Alex was laying flat on his stomach over the hole, staring down into the pitch-black void.

"Is she conscious?" Dane asked first.

"Yes, she's crying."

"How deep is the well?"

"Twenty feet. Maybe a little more."

"Any water in it?"

"Accumulated rainwater, if anything. Most likely nothing."

"How'd this happen?"

From where she stood on the opposite side of the hole, Marilyn cried out, "It's my fault. All my fault."

Jessi wrapped an arm around Marilyn's shoulders and assured her, "No, it's not. I'm sure—"

"You don't understand," Marilyn wailed, "I was watching her. Alex was busy in the garage. She got up from her nap and came to sit in my lap. It was the first time she'd come to me like that. I was telling her we were going back to the park later to watch the fireworks. She was so excited."

Marilyn's tears came then, falling unheeded down her pale cheeks. "My mom called," she began again, "and while my back was turned Cissy took off. I figure she must have been trying to go back to the picnic. She saw the open field and went that way."

"Why wasn't this well covered?" Pike asked.

Alex looked up from his prone position on the ground. "It usually is. Kids come by and rip the cover off for fun. I keep replacing it. I hadn't been out here for a few days, though, and didn't realize it was missing."

A faint cry echoed up from the hole and Alex turned back to his daughter. "Daddy's right here, sprite."

Dane laid down on the ground beside Alex and flashed a heavy-duty flashlight down into the hole. Cissy's head was barely visible at the end of the stream of light.

"I can see her," Dane said. "I'd guess it's about twenty-five feet."

"Can we lower a man down into the hole?" Pike asked.

"I'll go," Alex offered.

"You wouldn't fit," Dane pointed out. "Then we'd have two rescues on our hands."

"What'll we do?" Marilyn asked.

Dane stood up and dusted off the front of his shirt, while he explained, "we'll do the only thing we can. We'll call for help."

Dane trotted back to the house and placed a call to the state police. They, in turn, patched him through to the nearest rescue unit attached to the Air National Guard in Grayling. After that, he called for heavy duty equipment and medical assistance.

Nearly half an hour later, Dane stepped out of the house and into the dwindling daylight.

"Well?" Jessi asked.

"There's a medical team on standby in Traverse City. They'll come as soon as the rescue begins. The closest heavy equipment I was able to locate is Grayling. As soon as he can round up his driver, they'll start over.''

''What about the Guard?'' she asked.

''The rescue team is being called back to duty. Most of the men were given time off for the holiday, leaving only a skeleton crew on the base. The whole team won't be reassembled until morning.''

''The morning?'' Jessi whispered. ''Cissy can't stay in that hole until morning.''

''It doesn't look as if we have a choice,'' Dane said resignedly, ''it's nearly dark now.''

Jessi followed Dane back to the well and stood by his side while he relayed the information to Alex, Marilyn, and the assembled crowd.

''No,'' Alex protested. ''She's scared and crying. It's damp and cold. Heaven only knows what damage the fall did. Something could be broken, or she could be bleeding internally. We can't leave her down there overnight. There must be something we can do.''

''I'd attempt the rescue myself if I thought I could make it,'' Dane assured him. ''But, like you, I'm too big. So's Pike.''

''But—''

Dane placed a consoling hand on Alex's shoulder. ''I'm sorry, man, there's just no other way.''

''Yes there is,'' Jessi said, her voice a moment of calm among all the excitement. When both Dane and Alex turned to her in question, she explained, ''I can fit. I'll do it.''

Fourteen

'No you won't,'' Dane argued.

"I couldn't ask that of you," Alex added, yet his eyes said something else entirely. He wanted her help.

Spurred on by the hope she could readily see in Alex's gaze, she insisted, "But I want to, and I can do it if you'll just let me." Peering over the edge of the opening, she told them, "I'm small enough. I'm strong enough. *And,*" she added for emphasis, "I'm all you've got."

Dane took Jessi by the hand and pulled her away from the crowd and behind a nearby tree. "It's too dangerous," he insisted.

"I'm not afraid."

"No," Dane said firmly.

"You don't think I can do it. Do you?"

"It's not that, Jess—"

Quickly, almost desperately, she interrupted, "I can do this. I know I can. Please let me try."

From behind them, Pike called out, "Dane, can I talk to you a minute?"

"Sure, I'll be right there." To Jessi, he said, "You stay right here." When she nodded, he turned to Pike and asked, "What is it, Ed?"

"Listen, Dane, I know how you feel about Jessi. And, I know where you're coming from in refusing her offer of help."

"Thanks, I need someone—"

"Not so quick," Pike countered. "I said I understood, not that I agreed."

"You can't be serious. I can't ask an untrained civilian to go down into that hole."

"Like she said, she's all we've got. Plus, she's not untrained. She's an athlete. Despite the fact that she hasn't competed in a few years, she's still in great physical shape."

"What if something happens?" Dane argued.

"What if nothing happens?" Life's full of *what-ifs*. You've said so yourself at least a thousand times."

"Yeah, but the what-ifs have never hit this close to home before." Shaking his head, he grumbled, "I can't let her do it."

Pike braced both hands on Dane's shoulders and stared straight into his eyes. "You can't eliminate the only hope we have because you want to protect her. She's a grown woman, Dane, and quite capable of making her own decisions."

"I know that, but I don't like it."

"Nobody said you had to like it, Dane." When Dane still didn't budge, Pike led him back to where Jessi waited, "Come on, let's get her tied off and ready."

"I can't believe I'm agreeing to this," Dane grumbled. "Not for a minute."

"Okay," Dane stated firmly, his gaze assessing Jessi's calm demeanor. "These are the rules. You get one try and one try only. We lower you with the ropes. Since the well is so narrow with a sloped bottom, you won't have room to stand. You also won't be able to bring Cissy up in your arms. That's why we have to lower you into the hole upside down."

"I know, it's the only plausible way."

Solemnly, Dane continued, "As soon as you reach Cissy, you tie off the extra rope like I showed you. You won't have much light to work with, only what the flashlight provides."

"I understand."

"We'll lower you about five feet and stop. Once you've adjusted to being upside down, tug on the rope two times and we'll let you down slowly. If at any time you think it might be too narrow, tug on the rope three times and we'll stop and pull you up. Got that?"

"Yes, I've got it."

Jessi sat down on the ground next to the gaping hole and pulled on the gloves Ed handed her. Kneeling beside her, Dane slipped the flashlight into the loop of her anchor rope and tightened the ends. In the next loop, he secured a walkie-talkie—her only method of communication once she entered the well. Their gazes met for a brief moment. Dane's expression was clouded with concern, and she offered him a smile.

"Don't worry, Dane. This can't be any more grueling than practicing ten to twelve hours a day."

He smiled back, but the gesture didn't erase his worry. "I suppose not, sweetheart. You take care, and don't do anything foolish."

"Not me," she assured him.

Double checking the relay switch on the walkie-talkie, he ordered, "Keep in touch."

Despite the crowd of people surrounding them, Dane leaned forward and pressed a kiss to Jessi's lips. She returned his kiss with equal fervor. When he lifted his head, he smiled. Reaching out, he switched on the flashlight and turned Jessie toward the well.

"Let's get this show on the road," Dane ordered.

As easily as a greased-down channel swimmer slips into the water, Jessi slid into the well. "There's a good foot on either side of me," she called back.

Dane breathed a sigh of relief and held fast to his side of the rope, feeding it slowly into the well. Alex manned the other rope and Pike the backup rope. At five feet they stopped, just as he had said they would, giving Jessi time to adjust to being upside down.

Within moments she was signaling them to continue.

Inside the hole, Jessi calmly told herself that there was nothing to worry about. Being topsy-turvy inside an old well was no worse than working the uneven bars, only darker. And, with Dane and the others as her support, nothing could possibly go wrong.

In the distance she could see Cissy, her small form illuminated by the flashlight's beam. The child's eyes were closed, yet she was rocking back and forth rather than sleeping. From what Jessi could tell, she didn't seem to be seriously hurt.

"Cissy?" Jessi called out softly.

"Yeth?"

Although soft and trembling, the response was everything Jessi had hoped to hear.

"It's me, Jessi. I'm coming to get you."

"Get me," she repeated. "Wanna see daddy. See Hawee, too."

"Yes, sweetie. I'll take you to see your daddy and Harley."

The sides of the well were made of stone, and slick with both water and mud. To Cissy's right Jessi could see fallen rocks where part of the well had caved in.

As Dane had predicted, the walls narrowed a bit about halfway down, then flared out again closer to the bottom. She needed to objectively assess her ability to pass through the narrowed section. Following Dane's instructions, Jessi tugged on the rope, signaling for the men to stop.

"What's wrong?" Alex asked in alarm. "Why's she stopping?"

"I'm not sure," Dane said, "I'll check and see."

Taking the walkie talkie from his back pocket, he pressed the relay button. "Jessi? Why are you stopping?"

Jessi braced one hand against the side of the well and, reaching up, depressed the radio's transmitter button. "It's narrowing a bit, like you said it would. I just want to make sure I can fit."

"Smart thinking, Jess," Dane commended. "Tug again when you're ready to move."

A warm drizzle fell slowly from the sky, all but the heaviest drops evaporating before they could hit the ground. "As long as the rain stays like this, it shouldn't pose a problem," Dane said absently, as much for his own benefit as for that of the others.

"What if it gets worse?" Alex asked.

Dane summoned up his most optimistic smile. "We'll worry about that *if* it happens."

Jessi finished her assessment of the opening, certain that she could fit through without problems. Tugging on the rope she started the lowering process once again.

Within reach of the well's bottom, Jessi's shirt caught on something sharp. The ragged edge lanced her side, and she stiffened in surprise. Her sudden, and unexpected, movements caused one of the ropes to tangle around her ankle and snag on an outrcropping of rock. The thick rope pulled hard on Jessi's leg, straining her bad knee. Pain shot through her so suddenly—so deeply—that she nearly passed out. Nausea washed over her, filling her throat with the bitter taste of bile, choking off her ability to cry out in pain.

" 'essi," Cissy called.

The little girl stretched out her arms in trusting supplication.

"Right here, honey." Biting back on the cry welling up in her throat, Jessi assured her, "I'll just be another minute."

Her hands shaking, Jessi reached for the radio, only to knock it out of its loop and into the pit below. Oblivious to her dilema, the men kept working, lowering the ropes slowly, bringing her closer to the bottom she could barely discern through her agony. With every ounce of composure she possessed, Jessi fought past the blinding pain and signaled for the men to stop.

She was about to reach out to Cissy when the little girl's hands came up and touched Jessi's face. "Cry? 'essi, cry. 'essi 'fraid."

"No, sweetie. Jessi's just a bit sore, and a lot tired."

"Cissy sore, too."

The walkie-talkie lay just beyond Jessi's reach. Signaling for a bit more rope, Jessi twisted and turned until she closed the distance between herself and the radio. Retrieving it, she pressed the button and asked, "Can anyone hear me?"

No answer came to her call.

"Can anyone hear me?" she repeated.

"You're breaking up, Jessi," Dane responded. "Is everything okay?"

"Yes. I'm tying off Cissy's ropes right now. I'll signal when we're ready."

Dane's voice came back at her again, garbled and barely understandable. In the foggy haze of her mind, Jessi could have sworn he'd said he loved her.

Don't be ridiculous. That's not something a man says over a walkie-talkie, in front of a dozen people.

"You're right," she said aloud, answering her inner voice.

"Right," Cissy echoed.

Dane waited anxiously for Jessi's signal. Everyone around him was doing their best to pretend they hadn't overheard what he'd said. Blurting out *'I love you'* like that—and over a walkie-talkie to boot—wasn't the most romantic way to tell someone you love them. Still, he'd meant what he'd said and wouldn't pretend it hadn't happened.

Ever since he'd helped Jessi into the well, he'd been cursing himself royally for agreeing to her rescue attempt. Then, when she'd stopped the ropes he'd nearly panicked and jumped in the damned hole after her. Finally, when she'd radioed that everything was fine, he'd cursed his stupidity for not having told her he loved her before now.

Hell, he'd known it for ages. Probably ever since he'd pulled her in off Abel's roof. She was replenishment to his bruised heart; a balm to his open wounds. She was heat when he needed it; and a breath of fresh air when he got too hot. Most of all, she was love. *His love.*

Her tugs on the rope drew him from his thoughts. As one, the three men pulled. Slowly, evenly, they drew Jessi and her charge to the surface. Behind them, half the town had gathered in the open field, all there to offer their silent prayers and support. Marilyn took charge of a tearful Harley, the two of them sitting inside the nearby patrol car.

The rain fell harder than before, making the ropes slick. As a precaution, Dane suggested they wrap the ropes around their bodies for leverage and to prevent slipping.

Jessi could feel the steady pull of the rope against her waist.

The rope that had been tangled around her leg and had caused her such pain, stretched taut beneath Cissy's weight. Jessi's leg was numb from ankle to thigh, yet she couldn't think about that now, not while she and Cissy were still inside the well.

They were coming up on the narrow section when Jessi realized something was wrong. Her foot kept banging against the side of the well, sending a pins-and-needles sensation through her thigh. It was then that she realized the seriousness of her injury. Bent at the angle it was, her leg would hamper their passage to the top. They'd be stuck. Or, if they were pulled through, her leg would be damaged far more than it already was.

Jessi signaled the men above her with three sharp tugs on the rope. As quickly as her next heartbeat, the ascent was halted. She glanced down at Cissy, the little girl's eyes shone back at her, brilliant with tears.

Think, Jessi, think.

Jessi tightened the hold of her left hand on Cissy's arm and crooned softly to the little girl to reassure her. Then, she lifted her right hand and slid it along her own side. Pressing as hard as she could against her hip, Jessi closed her eyes tight, forcing her leg straight.

The pain was overwhelming, yet still she pushed. After the third try, she felt movement in her hip and the return of the tingles in her feet. Saying a silent prayer of thanks, she tugged on the rope one time and they were moving once more.

They passed through the narrowed section with ease, and Jessi breathed a sigh of relief. Cissy held tightly to Jessi's shirt and buried her face in the side of Jessi's neck.

"It'll be just another few minutes or so, sweetie. Then we'll see daddy."

"Gonna see Hawee, too," Cissy said.

"Yes, Cissy, Harley, too."

Jessi's feet were barely visible above the lip of the well when the rumbling started through the crowd. Like an ocean wave, it roiled and grew, gathering strength with every foot it traveled. By the time Dane had secured his arms around Jessi's waist, and pulled her free of the hole, the entire crowd was cheering and wiping tears of joy from their eyes.

Unashamedly, Dane wiped the tears from his own cheeks, as well. Drawing Jessi to his chest, he held her suspended above the damp ground. Hugging her tightly, he kissed her over and over again, rejoicing in the knowledge that both she and Cissy were safe.

Alex grabbed his daughter from Jessi's arms. Leaning close to where Dane held Jessi aloft, he kissed her cheek and whispered his thanks.

"You're welcome, Alex," she mumbled.

Alex stepped back, hoisting Cissy up for all to see. Other than a few cuts and bruises, she seemed relatively unscathed. Another cheer went up, causing the little girl to giggle and clap her hands.

Off in the distance, the first of the fireworks exploded into the darkened night, a fitting end for the rescue operation.

"Daddy?" Cissy whispered.

"What is it, baby?"

"Gotta go pottie."

Dane grinned broadly and wrapped his arms around the woman he loved. It felt so good to have her safe. So wonderful to have her in his arms. Nuzzling close to her ear, he whispered, "Listen, sweetheart, I'm sorry I said what I said over the radio."

At her puzzled look, Dane realized how poorly he'd worded his statement. "I don't mean I didn't mean it, I only meant I wish I'd waited until you were safely in my arms. Something like that shouldn't be broadcast. At least not the first time."

Jessi's head was spinning like a child's toy top, her mind befuddled by Dane's strange words. "What are you talking about?" she asked. "What did you say?"

"Not much I guess, if you can't remember it," he teased. Setting her down on the ground, he started to repeat his words of undying love.

The moment Jessi's feet hit the ground, her leg buckled. By the time Dane repeated, "I love you, Jessi Trainor," she'd succumbed to the excruciating pain in her leg and crumpled at his feet.

* * *

Jessi woke up in a hospital bed, her leg encased in a fiberglass cast. Her room was filled with vases and baskets of flowers. Cards hung on every wall. Despite all the adornments, the only thing Jessi saw was Dane, his body slumped in a nearby chair, his head bent in sleep, his clothes rumpled. He looked good enough to eat.

Had she been able to negotiate the bed, she would have loved waking him up with a kiss. Instead, she settled for watching him sleep.

The silence in the room was soothing, broken only by the occasional muffled sound that Jessi thought might have been the beginnings of a snore. She closed her eyes, not to sleep but to reminisce.

It was amazing how quickly both the town, and its inhabitants, had grown on her. She'd known, from Karen's initial description, Brant Mills would be beautiful. She hadn't been disappointed.

As she had so often over the past few months, she wondered what her time in Brant Mills would have been like had it not been for that odius man and his expensive raincoat. Had she not gone to the sheriff's office, would she have met Dane anyway? Somehow, she thought so. As right as it felt loving Dane Logan, she couldn't picture not knowing him.

Most importantly—well, maybe second to Dane—was that fact that she'd been able to face her ghosts, and put her past behind her. While she'd certainly never compete again, and never coach on an advanced level, she still had the knowledge and the ability to train the beginners—the children who trusted her implicitly with their minds and their bodies.

She, in turn, had entrusted them with her heart.

Last, but certainly not least, was her confidence in herself. No longer would she feel inadequate. There may be a time when doubts would surface, but Jessi knew she'd overcome them. She knew, with Dane's love, and her own self-confidence, she'd defeat any obstacle—no matter how threatening. And, if she ever felt overwhelmed, all she had to do was close her eyes and replay the cheers of the crowd when she and Cissy were pulled safely from the well. More precious than any applause she'd earned during competition, the love she'd felt in those few moments enveloped her. Protected her. Encouraged her.

Dane shifted restlessly in the chair, drawing her from her thoughts and back to the reality of his presence. When his eyes opened, she met his gaze.

"Good morning, sleepyhead," she teased.

"Me? You're the one whose slept like Rip Van Winkle."

"I have?" she asked. Suddenly it dawned on her that she had absolutely no idea what time it was, or what day it was, for that matter.

"Two days, to be exact. The doctor said it was nothing to worry about, and that your body was only replenishing itself."

"Two days?"

"Yes, and you have at least a few more days in the hospital, followed by more rest at home, and then therapy."

Jessi pressed her palm against the cast, letting Dane's words sink in.

As if he could read her thoughts—her worries—Dane explained, "There's no permanent damage. Torn ligiments and a compound fracture."

"I wasn't sure. When I felt the initial stab of pain, I thought it was only a pulled muscle."

Dane drew a hand through his hair, rearranging it in a haphazard way Jessi found most endearing, and definitely sexy. His smile, so prevelant before, turned suddenly into a frown.

"Why didn't you say something, Jess? If we'd known you were hurt—"

"There wasn't anything we could do about it then," she pointed out. "I was less than ten feet from Cissy. It wouldn't have made any difference, and no sense, to pull me up before I had her."

"The doctor says the pain must have been intense."

She shook her head, denying the truth in hopes of saving Dane some unnecessary worry. "Not so bad. Compared to the original injury, this was mild."

She could tell by the skepticism in his eyes he didn't believe her, but he said nothing. Jessi leaned forward and reached for Dane's hand. Lifting his hand to her mouth, she brushed the back of his knuckles with her lips and pressed a lingering kiss to his palm. He sucked in a deep breath and held it, his eyes closed. A muscle in his jaw twitched, and his pulse beat visibly in his throat.

"I'm sorry I caused you so much trouble," she told him.

"Anxiety was more like it," he corrected. "I can't ever remember being so scared as I was when we lowered you into that hole."

"You really didn't think I could do it, did you?"

It was his turn to take her hand in his. When he drew her fingertips to his mouth, her hand was trembling. "I had no doubt you could make the rescue, Jessi. The only doubts I had were in myself. I suddenly realized that I'd willingly sent you into that damp, dark hell-hole without ever telling you how much I love you."

"And—exactly—how much is that?"

"More than you'll ever know."

"Really?"

"Well, maybe not," he conceded. "If I start now, and tell you five times a day for the next forty or so years, that might do it."

"Just forty? I plan on having you around for a whole lot longer than that, Dane Logan."

"Then, I guess it's a given that you'll marry me."

"I'm not sure. I mean that wasn't exactly the most romantic proposal I've ever heard."

Laughing, he told her, "It's a far sight better than the first one I gave you."

"First? Did I sleep through it?"

"Kind of," he admitted. "You were in the back of the ambulance, and nearly unconscious."

"Then, it doesn't count. A woman has to be lucid and otherwise indisposed for the proposal to count."

Dane shrugged, then drew a deep breath as if contemplating an unsurmountable task. Dropping to one knee in melodramatic style, he asked, "Jessi Trainor, will you do me the honor of being my wife?"

Imitating his shrug and his deep sigh, she told him, "I suppose so, but there is one thing . . . "

He waited, more patiently than she would have given the circumstances.

"Well?" he prompted.

"You snore."

"I do not."

"Yes you do. I heard you with my own ears. How do you ever expect me to sleep?"

Dane's smile spread, his eyes twinkling with mischievousness. "That's the whole idea, sweetheart. I don't."